HARMONY'S SONG
and
OTHER STORIES

HARMONY'S SONG and OTHER STORIES

Carl Wooton

Copyright © 2018 by Carl Wooton.

Library of Congress Control Number: 2018907865
ISBN: Hardcover   978-1-9845-3956-4
           Softcover   978-1-9845-3957-1
           eBook   978-1-9845-3958-8

All rights reserved. No part of this book may be reproduced or transmitted in any form or by any means, electronic or mechanical, including photocopying, recording, or by any information storage and retrieval system, without permission in writing from the copyright owner.

This is a work of fiction. All of the characters, names, incidents, organizations, and dialogue in this novel are either the products of the author's imagination or are used fictitiously.

Any people depicted in stock imagery provided by Getty Images are models, and such images are being used for illustrative purposes only.
Certain stock imagery © Getty Images.

Print information available on the last page.

Rev. date: 07/26/2018

To order additional copies of this book, contact:
Xlibris
1-888-795-4274
www.Xlibris.com
Orders@Xlibris.com
779103

CONTENTS

Arrangements 1
Ramblers and Spinners 10
The Tick Is Full 33
All in a Day's Work 56
The Chill 66
A Wide Day 78
When the Trumpet Sounds 97
Picking Up the Pieces 111
A Boy in the Woods 123
That Summer Day 135
Harmony's Song 147

To Dolores

The stories published here stem from fifty years of writing and teaching. They all have been previously published in journals and anthologies from 1965 to 2018. I owe too many people so much, but some must be mentioned with a great sense of gratitude: Ray Mouton, Nancy Richard, David Kann, Marcia Gaudet, Ann B. Dobie, Ernest J. Gaines, Jeanne Voelker, and a multitude of others who read many drafts, corrected my many mistakes, and most of all, encouraged me to keep going through difficult times.

ARRANGEMENTS

WALTER MEIER CRUSHED the cigarette in an ashtray on the small table beside his bed and listened to the distant thunder and the whisper of the first drops of rain falling against the window screens. Through the streaks of light suggested by the near dawn, he saw Elizabeth lying half-uncovered on the bed. Her light-brown hair spread on her pillow. In the faint light, he thought how her perfectly smooth face was untroubled and childlike. The soft rise and fall of her breathing blended with the brushing sound the soft rain made against the windows. Elizabeth turned in the bed so that he could no longer see her face clearly, but he knew it was peaceful, maybe even smiling.

He looked at the luminous dial of the clock on the dressing table. He was disappointed to see that it was only five o'clock. The appointment with the county medical examiner was not until nine thirty.

Four years earlier, Walter thought of himself as not unhappy. He had a good job traveling over the southern half of the state, selling shoes to retail outlets. He had money in a savings account that he planned to use for an extended trip to Europe, a new car every odd year, and freedom. He had no responsibilities and no ties, except to the job, and he planned—when the savings account became large enough—to be free of it. He had no health problems, except for occasional severe headaches that made him forgetful, but only of small and insignificant things. Generally, *things* were good. His life was thoroughly planned, and the plan pleased him. Then he met Elizabeth.

It was at an outdoor party in May. He talked to her only briefly then, but during the following week on the road, he discovered himself remembering her. When he returned to town on Friday, he called her; and on Sunday, they went for a ride through the pinewoods that bordered a nearby lake. After that weekend, he planned his route to allow him to be in town every weekend. They took trips to the lake or they drove to the Gulf Coast to eat shrimp caught fresh that same day.

For Walter, the weekdays became unreasonably protracted periods of anticipation. He spent the nights away from Elizabeth alone in motels, and he often lay on his bed in the darkness and listened to the sounds—laughter and music and voices of people not alone—that penetrated the walls of his room. Late at night there would be nothing, and the dark emptiness of his room evoked an unremitting terror in the thought that she might not be at the apartment on Friday. He needn't have worried. She was there, every weekend, waiting for him. They married late in August.

At the end of the first year, they bought a house. He tried then, as he had tried before, to persuade her to stop working, but she showed him that it would be impractical. He did not feel strongly about the point; it was not worth a conflict, and he let her easily overcome his objections. His life continued to seem well planned. He was home every Wednesday night, in addition to weekends. The miles between towns and motel rooms were no longer empty; he filled them with a mixture of memories of the weekend before and anticipation of the weekend to come. He carried a small framed picture of her in his suitcase. Each night away from home, he put it on a table in the motel room; it made the darkness less empty.

He considered his marriage a success. Walter thought, during the second year and the third, that their relationship grew firmer daily. They liked and disliked the same things and the same people. They read the same books, and often, it seemed to him that they thought exactly the same thoughts. There were no apparent causes of conflict between them, and there were only a few things that even mildly bothered Walter.

One of them was something that was never mentioned. He hoped for children or, at least, a child, but Elizabeth seemed not to care. She never had so much as hinted that she did not want a child, but she puzzled him by failing, also, to mention any hope of having one. He had started to ask her about it several times, but each time, he had remained silent. He did not want to intimidate her.

Another thing that once bothered him was something he found he could now laugh at, even while it bothered him. He knew from the first time he met her that Elizabeth previously had been married and divorced. A friend introduced her to him as Elizabeth Guillory MacLaughlin. He had expected when they married that she would drop her first husband's name. She insisted, however, on signing her name as Elizabeth Guillory MacLaughlin Meir. He did not understand it, but she insisted; finally, he dismissed it as just another example of the strangeness of female vanity.

The clock on the bedroom dressing table showed nearly six, and the sudden daylight pierced the window and fell on Elizabeth's face. She stirred, and Walter stood and drew the curtains in order to allow her to sleep the few minutes remaining until the alarm would ring. He went into the bathroom, took his shaving equipment from the medicine cabinet, and turned on the hot water. A few minutes later, the alarm briefly rang in the bedroom. He finished shaving and went into the bedroom; Elizabeth was not there. He found her in the kitchen. She was making coffee and turned toward him as he came into the room.

"Sleep well? No, I don't suppose you did. I'll have your breakfast ready in a minute. It's drizzling outside."

"It rained hard earlier," he said.

"How long have you been up?"

"Not long."

The lie passed unremarked; it was part of the game they had been playing for a while. She had refused to become disturbed, or even to notice that anything was wrong. Walter thought it seemed as though she had made a rule: *nothing must upset Walter*. Of course, Walter knew it was an impossible rule to follow; even Elizabeth sometimes forgot.

A little more than six months earlier, Walter made three calls in towns close together by noon, and after a quick lunch, he began the ninety-mile drive to his next stop at the edge of his territory. A recent rain had left the highway wet, and the tires of the car hissed monotonously. He developed a severe headache, and the pain and the wet highway caused an optical illusion. An oncoming truck appeared in Walter's lane, and he swerved to avoid it. The jar of the wheel dropping off onto the right shoulder of the highway shattered the illusion, and Walter jerked the car back onto the road. The headache spread until it felt as though something had hit him hard at the base of his skull. The road seemed to undulate, and the long white line in the center trembled like a thin painted snake. Then there was nothing except a distant, thin hissing sound of tires on wet pavement and motion and pain.

He awoke in a motel room unfamiliar to him. It was small, and smelled of mildew. The furniture was old and scarred. He dressed quickly and packed his suitcase that lay open on the floor at the foot of the bed; he noticed that Elizabeth's picture had remained face downward in the suitcase. Fear and panic surged through him. Outside the room, he failed to recognize the name of the motel. The fear swelled as he drove out of the parking lot and turned onto the highway. He failed to recognize the highway or any of the buildings along it. He drove a mile, and then he saw a sign that marked the city limits of a town more than two hundred miles from his home and nearly sixty miles outside his territory. As he drove through the town, he noticed the shops and stores were closed. The town seemed almost deserted. Then suddenly, a crowd appeared in front of him; people poured from a church and spilled for a moment into the street. It was Sunday. From Thursday to Sunday, he remembered nothing, how or why he came to be where he was, what he did, whom he saw: *nothing*.

The crowd from the church dispersed and left the street clear. He drove on until he saw a telephone booth. He stopped and called Elizabeth collect.

Her voice said, "Where are you?"

Walter blurted out what had happened to him, He was afraid she would be greatly upset. He knew his own terror was apparent in his voice. He waited, but she said nothing.

"Are you there?" he asked.

"Yes. Don't worry."

The soft calmness of her voice surprised him. There was another long silence. He wanted her to say something more, to reassure him, to tell him what to do. He held his breath and listened for the sound of her breathing, to make certain she still was there. Finally, he could wait no longer for the suggestion he had wanted her to make.

"I'm leaving now to come home."

"All right. I'll be here."

Her voice was almost whisper-soft and distant. It seemed strangely detached, like the voices of the recorded messages of time and weather that can be dialed on the telephone. Walter felt foolish for having bothered her.

He said, "I'm leaving now. Goodbye."

"Goodbye. Drive carefully."

"Yes. All right."

It was a long trip. He spent every mile trying to discover, in some inarticulate part of his memory, what had happened between Thursday and Sunday. As he drove, he thought he caught an occasional glimpse of some fragment—a face, a town, the interior of a strange room, a voice—that, for a moment, seemed real. But it soon dissolved into the scenes rushing past the window or in the sound of the car on the highway. Those few images that lingered longest became strangely isolated in his mind—dreamlike shadows entirely without context, almost spectral. It was nearly dark when he arrived home. Elizabeth was waiting; she was kind to him and, he thought, amazingly undisturbed.

He did not go on the road the following week. On Monday, he saw a doctor—a general practitioner. On Thursday, he saw a psychiatrist. For a few weeks, things seemed to go well. He worked, but he added a week to the period it usually took him to make all the calls in his territory. He spent one hour a week talking to the psychiatrist, a Dr. Bergeron, who seemed both compassionate and understanding. Elizabeth remained calm and unalarmed. She refused to talk about what had happened; she made his worrying seem almost childish.

Then it happened again. He awoke in a strange motel room in a strange town more than a hundred miles outside his territory, and with no memory of what had happened from Thursday morning to Sunday. He hired a high school boy he found on the street to drive him home, and then he paid the boy's return trip on the bus. On Monday, the psychiatrist suggested Walter be committed to the state hospital for closer supervised therapy. That was a week ago. Today Walter and Elizabeth were to see the county medical examiner to complete the required papers.

Walter and Elizabeth arrived early at the medical examiner's office. They had to sit on opposite sides of the crowded waiting room. Walter looked carefully at each of the other persons in the room, and he wondered if any of them knew why he was there. When his glance came again to Elizabeth, he found some comfort in the way she was able to appear perfectly composed. Even during the last week, she had remained the picture of calm. He wondered what thoughts might be going through her mind. She had remained quiet during the drive from the house, speaking only once and then only to complain about the rain. He had wanted to say something to her or to hear her speak, anything right then to reassure him of the strength of their marriage, but she had remained silent and at ease.

The door at the end of the waiting room opened, and a young nurse appeared and called their names. They rose and went through the door, following the nurse along a green-walled corridor and into an office.

"The doctor will be with you in a moment," the nurse said, and then she left them alone in the office.

The room was small. A large desk and a chair, two extra chairs, a small table, a filing cabinet, and a narrow bookcase were crowded into it. A half dozen potted plants made the room seem even smaller than it was. The air was oppressive, and Walter wished he had stayed in the larger waiting room.

Elizabeth asked, "Are you all right?"

Walter looked at her and put his hand on her arm to show her his gratitude for her expression of concern. He thought all this must be extremely difficult for her, although she certainly hid the fact well. He leaned toward her, but before he could speak, the door opened. The doctor in a white jacket and with a stethoscope hanging from his neck greeted each of them and sat behind a large desk.

"You understand that this is merely a formality."

He said it simply, seeming to speak to neither of them, and he gave no indication that he expected a reply. He continued talking. Walter tried to listen, but he found himself distracted by the few medical instruments evident in various places about the room. He puzzled over the coldness that seemed to emanate from the various tools designed to improve the well-being of humankind. The doctor stopped talking and pulled a number of printed forms from a drawer. He laid them carefully on the desk and pushed a button by the telephone. A buzzer sounded somewhere in the rear of the building.

The doctor said, "You will have to complete these forms. My nurse will help you."

The office door opened again, and the nurse came into the room. She smiled at Walter. He thought he sensed that she understood and sympathized. The way she smiled suggested a compassionate interest that contrasted sharply with the impersonal efficiency suggested by the starched neatness of the white uniform.

The nurse said, "Will you come with me, please?"

Walter and Elizabeth followed the nurse to the end of the hall into a room lined with filing cabinets. Above the cabinets, the green walls were bare. In the center of the room was a large table; a typewriter was placed at one end of it. The nurse pointed to two straight chairs in front of the table. Walter and Elizabeth sat, and the nurse took her place at the typewriter. She put the first form in the typewriter.

"Who's going to answer the questions?"

Walter looked at Elizabeth. "You better," he said.

"All right."

It took only a few minutes to complete the first set of questions, with Elizabeth providing the answers. Walter, however, had to answer the questions asked by the next form; they asked about his schooling, his previous work experience, and his medical history—all things that had occurred before he had met Elizabeth. She would not know them; they had never mentioned the past. Life began at an outdoor party in May only four years earlier.

The doctor stepped into the room and asked Elizabeth to come into his office for a moment. Walter was left alone with the nurse and the inquiring forms. The nurse spoke to Walter without looking up from the form in her typewriter.

"I'm sure you'll like it at the hospital. It's really a nice place. I used to visit my uncle there."

She took the forms from the typewriter and inserted another set.

"You saw Dr. Bergeron about six months ago for the first time?"

"Yes," Walter answered.

"Don't you like him? He's so kind. He's much nicer than the one who cared for my uncle."

"Did your uncle get better?"

She seemed not to hear him. She located the card that contained the remaining information required by the form. She typed busily for several minutes.

When she stopped, Walter again asked, "Did your uncle get better?"

She did not look at him when she answered.

"Oh no. His wife divorced him, and just when the doctors thought he might soon come home."

She pulled the forms from the typewriter and spent a few minutes checking and arranging the completed papers before she stood.

She said, "Now we need the doctor's signature, and your wife will know what to do after that."

Walter felt uncomfortable as he stood and started toward the door. He had thought that, at this point, he would feel some amount of relief—but instead, he was more frightened than he had been when he first arrived at the office. As he reached the door, he turned to the nurse. She tried to step past him, but he placed a hand on her arm and stopped her.

"What happened to your uncle?"

She tried to walk away from him, but he closed his hand on her arm and stopped her. "What happened to your uncle?"

She said, "He had a permanent relapse when he heard about the divorce. Now we'd better find the doctor."

Walter let his hand fall and stepped aside to allow her to go before him into the hall. In hurrying, she accidentally brushed against him, and the papers fell to the floor. He stooped, picked up the papers, arranged them neatly, and handed them to her.

As she took the stack from him, he spoke, softly but urgently, "What is your uncle's name?"

The nurse had no opportunity to reply. The door to the doctor's private office opened, and Elizabeth and the doctor stepped into the hall. Elizabeth was smiling. The doctor took the forms from the nurse, placed them against the wall, and signed them. He walked with Walter and Elizabeth to the waiting room. As he came to the end of the hall, Walter turned around and looked for the nurse, but she had disappeared.

Outside the building, the rain still fell lightly. Walter walked behind Elizabeth, watching her step gracefully 'round the black pools forming on the sidewalk. The wetness dripped down the back of his neck and sent a chill through him. He felt the moistness increasing in the clenched palms of his hands, and he realized the moisture he felt was caused by cold sweat and not rain.

At the car, Elizabeth placed a hand on his arm and opened the car door for him. He looked at her standing in the rain. The water beaded on her face and fell into the black pool about her feet. She was smiling. As he looked into her eyes, their calmness and her smile faded into obscurity behind the curtain of rain falling more rapidly between them. A new unfamiliar horror attacked his senses, and the sound of the rain heightened to a painful intensity, and all that he saw suddenly was grotesque and threatening. He stumbled through the water and hid his face in his hands, wishing for the safety of real and silent darkness.

The car backed out of the parking place and went forward into the street. Elizabeth was silent. Walter looked up at the grayness outside the car and knew it would rain the rest of that day and through the night. He did not try to think of what would follow the rain.

RAMBLERS AND SPINNERS

IT SNOWED ALL day the Monday after Thanksgiving. After supper and homework, my brother, Will, and I sat in the narrowly opened window of the second-floor apartment where we lived. From there, we watched the older kids ride their bicycles down Sweet's Hill and hit their brakes at the corner beneath us and do four or five spins until they ended up in the next block in front of the Hoosier Café.

Bradshaw Morgan got more spins than anyone else did. He never got less than four, sometimes six—and once, although I didn't see it, he got nine complete spins.

Jerry McCloskey, a fat kid, came off the bottom of the hill, hit the corner, spun, and went down sprawling—the bike going one way, him another. The others helped him up, but not without a couple of them slipping and falling on the packed snow.

I laughed and said, "I can do better than that."

Will said, "Me too."

I said, "I bet I could get six spins, at least."

From behind us, our older sister, Angie, said, "Bet you can't."

Will and I didn't know she was there, watching us and listening to us. If we'd known, we sure wouldn't have said anything out loud. She came closer so she could watch Bradshaw Morgan and the other older boys. She was fifteen.

Will said, "I can."

She said, "You can't get six spins. You can't get any spins." Will was getting up to hit her. "You don't even have a bicycle."

The truth was more than Will could take, and he jumped at her. Angie yelled, and I grabbed Will and held him back. I really didn't care whether or not he clobbered Angie, but I knew if he did, I'd probably get the same punishment he did just for being there.

I sat on Will and told Angie, "You better get out while you can." She believed me and ran out of the room, calling for Momma.

I heard her say, "Will was trying to hit me," and Momma said, "Why don't you leave them alone when they're in there together?" I knew our father wasn't in the apartment. If he had been there, Momma would have said something like "Angie!" and our father would have been halfway down the hall already, coming to set things straight. Will struggled, and I got off him. He was strong for ten.

We went back to the open window, but the bicycle riders were all gone. The snow fell harder, and the freezing air that came through the open window made my eyes water, but I didn't close the window. The streetlight standing kitty-corner from our building shone on the tracks made by the bicycles. The falling snow was filling in the tracks, but I could see them as though they were still being made, as though Bradshaw Morgan was still spinning down the street toward the café.

Momma came into the room and said, "Shut that window, you two. You'll catch your death. I swear!"

Will shut the window.

I said, "I need a bicycle."

She said, "You got a money tree?"

Will said, "They don't cost much."

I said, "You won't have to get us nothing else for Christmas."

She said, "Get to bed. We'll talk about it later." She said it in the tone of voice she used when she meant the discussion was closed.

Will said, "I'm going to ask Daddy."

She said, "He's got enough trouble without you bothering him about some bicycles we can't afford. Get to sleep. You've got school tomorrow."

After she shut the door, Will said, "Do you think we can get a bicycle for Christmas?"

I said, "We don't have a prayer."

He said, "I'm going to ask Daddy."

I wrote off any hope of finding bicycles beside the Christmas tree that year. I had heard enough talk about signs of coming hard times. Momma, in fact, had already said something about there being nothing but foolishness in wasting good money on a tree we'd just have to throw out. But Momma's talking didn't touch Will. Only a couple of nights later, Will was true to his word about asking our father for the bicycles. If I'd paid a little more attention to him, I might have expected him to do it, but I never would have thought he would do it when he did.

He did it at grace. Whenever our parents had had a few days in a row without arguing about whether or not we were going to end up in the poorhouse, our father offered grace before supper. He never said anything more than thanks for good food and good health, but he ended it by indicating each of us should offer some kind of petition. My mother prayed for comfort for those mothers who had lost their sons in the war and for President Truman. Angie prayed for As on whatever tests she had to take that week. I asked for new tennis shoes and help in algebra. I wasn't worried about an A like Angie was. I just wanted help! Then Will, with his hands together and his fingers extended out straight, almost whispered, "Please let me and Mark get bicycles for Christmas."

He said it softly and with his hands up against his mouth. Our father reached over and lightly moved Will's fingers down.

He said, "I couldn't hear that, Will. Say it again, a little louder."

"Please let me and Mark get bicycles for Christmas."

Momma said, "Will! I told you we can't afford any bicycles."

Will didn't look at her. Neither did I. We both watched our father, half-expecting some kind of explosion that never came. He looked at Momma a half-second when she'd had her say and then looked back at Will, who still had his hands folded like he was thinking he had maybe better offer another prayer.

Then our father said, "What about Angie? Don't you want a bicycle for your sister?"

Will bowed his head further into his clasped hands and muttered, "And for Angie too."

Our father said "Amen," and there was a sound like someone blowing out candles on a cake. That was the first time I knew I had been holding my breath.

Momma mumbled something about people thinking they could pick money like apples, but she didn't make any more fuss during supper about Will's prayer. Nor did she say anything when Will asked again for bicycles for Christmas at supper every day the rest of that week. But that Sunday afternoon, I heard her talking to our father in the kitchen.

Momma said, "You shouldn't have encouraged him to go on about bicycles. He's just going to be disappointed."

Our father said, "We'll see."

"See what?"

"Maybe we can work something out."

"You're wearing two sweaters because we can't afford to keep the heat turned up, and you think we can pay for bicycles? You got a special kind of garden where you grow your money trees? Where are you going?"

"Downstairs."

Our father's business was downstairs. He made venetian blinds and sold them wholesale. Momma kept the books. They talked all the time about the business, but always as though Angie, Will, and I were not there. Our father kept saying he thought things would pick up in the New Year. Momma said things about ostriches and fools with their heads in the sand. I didn't understand probably half of what I overheard, but I knew business wasn't good. That was why the heat was turned down and we had to wear long-sleeved shirts and sweaters in the apartment.

Momma didn't like for our father to work on Sundays, but he almost always did, unless they didn't argue or talk about how much things cost. Even I figured out that nearly every Sunday afternoon, she said something to him about money not growing on trees. He would be almost halfway down the stairs before she finished. Sometimes I wanted to ask her why she hadn't figured that out too. But I didn't ask her, partly because I was a little bit afraid she had.

There was no saying of grace before and hardly any talk during supper for most of the following week. Each meal grew sterner and more silent. I admit that even though I had refused to share Will's hope, I shared his dreams of descending Sweet's Hill at rocket speed and spinning through the intersection, and it seemed as though even the dreams were slipping through a crack at the edge of the stillness of those suppertimes. The only good thing about mealtime was the kitchen where we ate was still warm from Momma's cooking.

During that week, our father came late to the table, ate his meal, thanked Momma for fixing it, and went downstairs. Sometimes I heard him come back after we had gone to bed. He and Momma talked low late at night. I couldn't ever hear everything, but sometimes I heard him say things like, "I've got to believe we'll make it," and sometimes something like, "Christ, Goldie, I'm doing the best I can."

Near the end of the week, our father came to the table first and sat with his hands in his lap while he waited for the rest of us to settle in our places. Will was the last one to the table. He came hurrying, and as he sat in his chair next to mine, he flashed some kind of paper at me and shoved it into his hip pocket.

Our father prayed his grace, and he surprised us at the end of it by adding a new petition: "Please let the county commissioners act fairly when they award the contract for the new blinds at the old folks' home." His voice stumbled through it, as though he was embarrassed to be asking for anything more than good food and good health. He cleared his throat, and Momma followed with a prayer for all the poor people who wouldn't have a proper Christmas that year.

Then Angie said, "Please let us have bicycles for Christmas."

Momma made a noise, sucking in her breath. Will and I grinned and squirmed in our chairs, and our father stared at Angie and looked puzzled. Angie sat with her hands folded like she was imitating a statue of an angel. I didn't know what had possessed her, but I thought I had better be quick and follow her example.

I said, "Please, God, let us have bicycles for Christmas."

And Will said, "Please let me and Mark and Angie have a bicycle for Christmas."

Momma said, "Do you know how much a bicycle costs?"

Angie said, "Nineteen dollars and 95 cents. Will and I found some in the Sears catalog."

Will pulled the paper he had shown me from his hip pocket and handed it to Momma.

Will said, "There, at the bottom. I want a red one."

Momma said, "You ought not to tear pages out of my catalog without asking." She looked at the picture and said, "That's twenty dollars. Times three, that's sixty dollars. And that doesn't include carrying charges. We don't have that kind of tree." She ignored Will's open hand stretched toward her, folded the paper, and put it under her plate.

Our father said, "Goldie, let's wait and see."

Momma said, "We're wondering how we're going to pay for the next tank of butane, and you want to wait and see about some bicycles that nobody can pay for? I swear, Ernest. Sometimes I wonder."

She said that a lot, but she never explained exactly what she wondered about. Late at night, when we were in bed and couldn't sleep, Will and I used to guess, but we never did figure out just what she meant. That night, I didn't think I would ever go to sleep. Almost as soon as the light was out, Will said, "I bet we get them."

I said, "What made Angie come around to our side?"

He said, "Bradshaw Morgan."

"How's that?"

"I heard Ruth Ann Parker saying Bradshaw Morgan made Patsy Jukeman his girlfriend last summer because she had a bicycle and would go riding with him in the country—all the way to Raccoon Creek and the hogback—anytime he wanted her to."

Angie made no secret about wanting to be Bradshaw Morgan's girlfriend, but I was amazed Will had figured it out, even hearing what he did. He thought girls should be treated like poisonous insects, and he didn't waste much of his time worrying about how they thought. But he had understood Angie this time, and he knew as well as I that our father was not going to dismiss such a prayer from her lightly.

Will and I stayed awake until long after our parents had gone to bed. We whispered in the light from the streetlamp about all the places that we would go if and when we got our new bikes. Finally, Will stayed silent when I asked him a question, and all I could hear was the sound of a car crunching the snow in the street below and, after that, the soft murmur of our parents' voices circling in the dark, cold air. Then suddenly, our father's voice rose.

"Goddamn it, Goldie, all I said was we'll wait and see."

Then it was quiet for a few minutes until their voices and the sounds of them moving around came down the hall again. It was like the thinness of the cold air offered no resistance to the sounds they made, and I pulled my three blankets tighter around me. The cold air and the darkness moved together around my head, and I had a vision of Bradshaw Morgan waiting for me in front of the Hoosier Café as I came down Sweet's Hill, hit a new glazing of ice in the intersection, and went into a string of acrobatic spins that awed even Bradshaw. I was almost into the last spin right in front of the café when I heard Momma's voice get almost loud, and she said, "Ernest! No! It's too cold!"

* * *

Will had to make a Christmas list at school. He printed his name at the top of his paper and the words *a red bicycle* in the middle of the page. He told Angie about it, and she helped him to make others—some with his name at the top, some with hers, and some with mine. They all had the single item, *a bicycle*, as the total Christmas shopping list for each of us. We taped copies on the doors to our rooms, on the wall beside the bathroom mirror, and even on the bulletin board downstairs in the office of the venetian blind business.

We got a tree, but we got it less than a week before Christmas, after they were marked down. It was small, barely as tall as Will, because Momma said, "A big tree wouldn't look good with only one string of lights." We made chains of colored construction paper and hung peppermint canes on the branches. Momma always saved the thin metal ribbons that she peeled off the tops of coffee cans. We twisted them and hung them to shine like shook tinsel when the lights were turned on. And in the last days before Christmas, we watched our parents' every expression and listened for hints in their inflections. At night, Will and I speculated about the meanings of their smallest gestures. He believed a Christmas bicycle was a sure thing. I agreed that, all in all, the signs were good. I did not share his faith, but since Angie's prayer, I had begun to hope.

On Christmas morning, we woke to the sound of our father yodeling in the kitchen. Sharp, heavy odors of fresh coffee and biscuits and bacon filled the warm air. When I threw off the covers, I knew Momma had turned up the thermostat. She was waiting outside the door when Will looked to see if there was a clear way to the living room.

Momma said, "Breakfast first."

She told us that was her father's rule when she was a little girl. She called it a family tradition. There was no point in arguing against it. We ate as quickly as we could, and we believed our parents deliberately took a great deal more time than they ever did with any other meal. But finally, breakfast was done, and our father and Momma went into the living room to prepare for us. We crept along the hall as far as we dared in order to be as close to the living room as we could be when they called for us. Then our father yelled "Come on!" and Momma shouted "Don't run!" We nearly leaped the last short distance into the room.

Joy! Joy! The purest joy I had ever known. Three bicycles stood in front of the tree. Our parents stood to one side, and Momma tried to take a picture at the instant of our amazement. Amazement and joy! Hope fulfilled! Each bicycle had a large sign taped to the handlebars to show whose it was. Will's and Angie's were red, and mine was a bright and glistening blue, like a clear sky reflected in water.

Will flipped up the kickstand on his bike, jumped on the seat, and started riding down the hall with Momma yelling and chasing after him. I followed, but Momma turned us both around and pushed us back into the living room. We had to open the rest of our presents, the ones that had come in the mail from relatives—sweaters, books, socks. One at a time, each had a turn. There were cards with notes about how sorry they were we lived so far away from everybody. And the bicycles stood at the entrance to the hall, ready, their clean lines defining speed and flowing spins on the icy streets that waited for us outside. Then, after the last package of more clothes from Grandpa Rambler, we were ready to go outside. Momma forced us into extra shirts and heavy coats and gloves with warnings not to stay out too long—especially Angie—because it was bitter cold. Our father helped us carry the bikes downstairs.

I wanted to go straight to the top of Sweet's Hill and come down to the intersection, but Angie and Will wanted to ride around town and make sure everybody saw our new bikes. I fussed, but I went with them. It couldn't take more than ten or fifteen minutes to ride past every block in town, and it didn't take a genius to figure out what Angie really wanted was to ride past Bradshaw Morgan's house. By the time we got back to the corner at the bottom of Sweet's Hill, we had a group of kids who wanted to ride down the hill and do tricks in the street. Besides ours, some others also had new bikes. They all believed they had the bike that would one day break Bradshaw's record of nine spins on one ride. Halfway up the slippery hill, someone turned around and yelled, "Look."

Bradshaw Morgan stood at the base of the hill beside his old bike, talking with Angie. Then, in a minute, he started up the hill, and Angie rode off toward the Hoosier Café to wait for us. Patsy Jukeman, Ruth Ann Parker, and some other kids who didn't have bikes were there too.

There was no way up iced-over Sweet's Hill on a bicycle except to walk and push, slip and fall, push and crawl. Fat Jerry McCloskey led the way, and it looked like he spent as much time falling as he did pushing and walking. The sky was dirty gray, and it looked as if the snow ought to start again any time, except it was too cold to snow. The wind blew stronger at the top of the hill, and not even extra shirts and a mackinaw kept it from slicing all the way through me. Ruth Ann Parker's little brother, Timmy, went first. The rest of us followed, with Will and me somewhere in the middle of the order. One went, and the next one counted to ten before he went because nobody wanted a collision at the bottom. Will was in place, then suddenly, he was hurtling down the hill in front of me, and I was counting. "One thousand eight, one thousand nine—"

"Go!"

A hand pushed on my back, and the cold in the wind stung my eyes and took away my breath. I pedaled at first, then held the pedals in a coasting position because the wheels were turning too fast for me to keep up with them. The back wheel hit a rut, came out of it, and I thought I was going to fall, but somehow I stayed up and headed for the bottom of the hill. I looked toward the intersection and saw a blur of people and bikes standing around, keeping the center clear. Then I was there. I locked the brakes, turned the handlebars, and spun, two, three, and went down. My leg caught under the bike, and I skidded along the street until I crashed into the rear wheel of a parked car.

Someone lifted my bike off me and someone else helped me up and another voice yelled, "Look out!" Another rider spun through the intersection. This one did better than I had, at least four and a half good spins and without falling down. I saw Will on the other side of the street, standing next to Jerry McCloskey.

"How'd you do?"

Will said "I was awful" and held up one gloved finger.

Jerry said, "He's too light. There's nothing to keep him going. You turned too tight and ran into yourself."

I turned the handlebars of my bike and looked at the front wheel coming around and thought I understood what he meant.

Someone yelled, "Bradshaw!"

And we all looked up the street to see Bradshaw coming toward the intersection. Nobody understood how he seemed to come down the hill so much faster than everybody else. He turned his handlebars, locked his brakes, spun, spun again and again, and looked like he would have gone forever if he hadn't been too far to the side. He had to stop to keep from sliding into the steel posts that held up the metal awning in front of the café. Angie and all her friends jumped around him like he was some kind of war hero coming home, but they didn't impress Bradshaw. He right away started moving back toward the hill for another ride.

We tried again. Will didn't do any better, and I did worse, even though I didn't fall. We went again. Will got two, and I got a little more than three again. I didn't turn the handlebars so hard, but I leaned too far, trying to help the bike pull itself around, and went down even harder than I had the first time. I got up and inspected my bike. Just two spokes on the front wheel were a little bent, not enough damage to keep me off the hill. Bradshaw got six really big looping spins on his third time. He looked as smooth and graceful as a figure skater.

We had started toward the hill for another run when Angie caught up with us and said, "Momma says you've got to come."

She said it loud in front of everybody, and they all laughed.

I said, "Tell her after this one."

Angie pointed toward the building, and I looked up. The angle was wrong to see anything, but I knew Momma was standing at the corner window, waiting for us to show we were coming home. Everyone else looked up too, and they all laughed harder.

Angie said, "You better come." She turned away. Will followed her.

Jerry McCloskey said, "You better go home, Mark."

He said it like he was talking to a little kid. Bradshaw looked over Ruth Ann Parker's head at me and grinned.

I said, "I'll go when I'm ready."

We climbed the hill again, but this time I hung back so I'd be one of the last. Bradshaw was always last. The wind blew harder. It had gotten colder. My face had almost no feeling in it. I went down the hill, and before I hit the bottom, I knew I was going to do better than three this time. I turned the handlebars, saw the lamppost go by twice and the bread box in front of the grocery store, three, four. I was going into five, and I could hear everyone yelling, and then I felt the bike go. I hit the iced pavement hard on my left arm, felt myself slide, and heard a scraping sound somewhere away from me. Everybody crowded into the street to see if I was hurt, and they kept Bradshaw Morgan, who never waited a full one-thousand-ten, from spinning at all.

My father came down and helped me home. Jerry McCloskey brought my bike. I kept trying to look at it while my father steered me toward the stairs at the back of the building. The handlebars were twisted out of line, and ends of broken spokes stuck out of the rims of both wheels. When they got it and me to the top of the stairs and stood my bike next to Will's and Angie's, mine looked like I had tried to destroy it.

My father said, "It'll probably be a while before I can fix it."

I might have said something if it had been just him and me on the landing, but I didn't say anything because Momma already had hold of my good arm and was pulling me into the kitchen. The warm air picked at my face and made little needles run up and down in my hands and feet. As soon as she decided my left arm wasn't broken, she made me drink a cup of hot cocoa. I waited for her to say something about the bike and about my not coming in when she had said for me to, but she didn't say anything. She just told me to go on and be easy the rest of the day because I had had enough of being out in the cold. I didn't argue, and I really didn't mind that the rest of the day turned out to be sort of like a thousand other days I remembered staying inside because it was too cold.

In bed that night, Will said, "You did great!"

Momma turned the thermostat down again, and the sound of the wind blowing down from the top of Sweet's Hill made the cold air in the apartment feel even thinner and sharper than usual.

Momma said, "I swear! A brand-new bike torn up the first day he rides it. And it's not even paid for!"

I heard our father say "I can fix it, Goldie. I'll get some spokes when I go to Terre Haute for the county commissioners' meeting."

The wind brought an ice storm the day after Christmas. The temperature went below zero and stayed there for the rest of the school vacation days. The roads in and out of town were impassable, so my father could not go to Terre Haute and get the spokes he needed to fix my bike. It did not matter much because Momma wouldn't have let us out to ride anyway. Neither, it seemed, would anyone else's momma. Will and I spent a lot of time looking out the window, waiting to see who would dare the hill with all the new ice and snow on it, but no one came. Not many cars tried the streets. There was nothing outside except the whiteness of the frozen snow that covered everything and the cold, cold air we felt when we got too close to the glass of the windowpane.

We had been back in school a couple of weeks when Momma told us the snowplows had finally cleared the roads, and she and our father were going the next day to Terre Haute to meet with the county commissioners. She told us in the evening because she wanted us to pray the commissioners would make a right decision about the blinds for the old folks' home. I left that up to Angie and Will and thought really hard all night and all the next day about our father buying the spokes for my wheels. I even tried to think of ways to get out of basketball practice after school in order to get home in time to help him repair the bike.

It was already dark when I left the gym. Running was nearly impossible on the icy streets and sidewalks, but I ran when I wasn't sliding. I stumbled up the stairs to the landing. My father knelt beside my bicycle, and he was fitting the last spoke into place. He had thick hands with short fingers that made him look clumsy when he worked with small things, but he inserted the spoke without any trouble. He stood and handed me the bike. The spokes in the wheels were all in place; the handlebars were straight. It was almost like Christmas morning all over again. I wanted to take it right then and ride through the streets to show everyone my bike was fixed, and I was ready for the next run down Sweet's Hill.

Momma had heard me on the stairs, and she opened the door to the kitchen and said, "Supper's ready. We're waiting for you." The others had already taken their places at the table by the time my father and I got there.

Our father prayed thanks for guiding the county commissioners, and I knew that meant he got the order for the blinds at the old folks' home. Momma said something about hoping we would use our blessings right. I don't remember what Angie and Will prayed for, but I gave thanks for the fixing of my bicycle and asked for the weather to get better. Then I realized we were having a Sunday dinner in the middle of the week, with dessert. Two freshly baked pies rested on the counter next to the stove. Our parents laughed and talked through the whole meal. They told us about the meeting with the county commissioners. Our father gave a detailed description of buying the spokes for my bicycle, and Momma made sure I understood how much trouble he had had putting them in my wheels so I could be surprised when I got home from basketball practice.

She said, "I hope you'll take better care of your bike now. It isn't made for doing acrobatics."

She stopped short of forbidding me to ride with the others down Sweet's Hill. She did warn me of "dire consequences" if I played what she considered the fool again. I understood that if she thought I wasn't careful enough, I'd be walking for the rest of my foreseeable life.

I said, "I'll be careful."

After Momma saw that our light was out and the door was closed, I got up, wrapped a blanket around me, and looked out the window at the intersection. It was dark. Someone had shot out the streetlight. The snow and ice were gray and looked colder than they did in the daylight. The chill came through the glass, and I hurried shivering back to bed and pulled up the extra quilt Momma had put at the foot. Will was snoring. Momma and my father were making the noises they always made when getting ready to go to bed, except they were talking and laughing more than they had in a long time.

Momma said, "Oh, Ernest!" Everything was real quiet until I heard Momma making sounds—sounds like little moans. Then those sounds stopped, and my father said, "Goldie, everything's going to be fine, just fine."

2

That winter broke every record it could for being cold. No one went out who didn't have to. We even got unexpected holidays from school, but ten or fifteen minutes outside drove the bravest and the foolhardiest alike inside. The bicycles stayed on the landing. Momma stayed downstairs almost as much as our father did. She even went with him after supper and on Sunday afternoons. We heard talk about trimming expenses and cutting back. The thermostat was turned even lower. Sometimes it seemed if one of us—Angie or Will or me—even looked like we might ask for something, Momma reminded us there were lots of different kinds of trees in the woods, but none of them grew money.

They brought the paperwork and bookkeeping upstairs to the kitchen table at night to save on heating costs downstairs. They talked about business. I didn't understand most of what they said, but I did understand that the order for the blinds at the old folks' home had not turned out the way they had hoped it would. And they argued about bills that had to be paid. They yelled at each other, apologized, and yelled some more. Our father became more and more silent, except when he worked on the books with Momma. He brought his silence even to the supper table, and if Momma sat like she was waiting to say grace, he didn't seem to notice and served food onto his plate. At times, he left the kitchen and went into the living room, sat in his big chair, and stared out a window, like he was seeing something none of us could see.

One afternoon early in February, there was no basketball practice, and I returned from school with Angie and Will. When we walked into the kitchen, Momma was wearing her heavy coat. Two suitcases stood by the door.

She said, "There's no heat. We're going to Terre Haute for a couple of days." And she named some people that she and our father knew who had agreed to take us in until somebody came and refilled our butane tank. Our father came in, picked up the suitcases, and walked out without saying a word. Momma pretended to look for something in a cabinet while he was in the kitchen. Then she made sure we had all our schoolbooks, pushed us out the door, and we all went downstairs to the car.

Before we got out of town, she asked, "Is there enough gas in the car to get there?"

Our father said, "Yes, goddamn it, Goldie. I'm not going to leave you stranded to freeze on the road."

"I didn't say you were. I didn't even think it."

"It's not my fault the gauge on the butane tank froze. It looked like we had plenty to last till next week. I would've paid the bill by then, somehow."

She said, "I'm not blaming you."

He said, "For Christ's sake, Goldie!"

Every morning, our father left the house where we stayed. When I asked Momma where he went, she said, "He's taking care of business."

He returned in the evenings, and they kept to themselves and whispered. Their friends seemed not to notice them. Will and I had to sleep on a pallet made of blankets on the floor. We were glad when, after nearly a week there, Momma told us we were going home the next day. The apartment was almost warm when we returned, and the first thing Momma did was turn the thermostat down.

The best thing was the weather came round to something more like normal. It was still cold, but it wasn't that wind-blowing, below-zero cold that kept almost every moving thing huddled in the warmest corner it could find. The sun was out most days, with the air bright and clear, and a couple of weekends after we were back, there was a real gathering at the intersection beneath our window. More than a dozen kids and some grown-ups looked toward the top of Sweet's Hill. Our father had come upstairs to see if we were going out.

Before I got my coat on, Momma said, "Keep in mind we can't afford to fix broken bicycles."

My father said, "Be careful."

On the way to the top of the hill, I felt all the excitement I had felt on Christmas Day. Everybody was happy to be out again. At the top of the hill, we heard the crowd at the bottom yelling at every rider. Halfway down the hill, I looked ahead at the intersection, and it was like I saw myself already there, making tight, rapid spins, not even needing to count them because the crowd was counting for me. The chill in the wind burned my face, and off the bottom of the hill, leveling out, I saw my father standing in front of his business. He was in shirtsleeves in the cold air, his hands pushed deep into his pockets as though that was all he needed to be warm. I had a flash of him kneeling on the landing, his hands holding the thin spokes of my wheels, and I did three easy spins and slid straight on toward the breadbox in front of the grocery store to keep from falling. I heard a murmur of disappointment from the crowd, and when I looked back toward the corner, my father had gone back into the building.

Will said, "What happened?"

I said, "Nothing."

Jerry McCloskey said, "He chickened out."

"Up yours, fatso!"

"You want to eat snow, dipshit?" He looked around for somebody to hold his bike.

It might have come to something big, fat McCloskey sitting on me and grinding me through the ice and snow into the pavement, but it stopped because the next rider down the hill lost control of his bike and came crashing into both of us and a half dozen others as well. By the time we got ourselves up, Bradshaw was at the bottom of the hill, and we forgot about everything except watching him. It was almost miraculous. Six, seven, eight, and he would have done the mythical nine and more if a car had not turned toward us at the next corner.

McCloskey and I had completely forgotten what had almost started between us, and nobody else even remembered we were there. We had eyes and thoughts only for Bradshaw. He had challenged us with something much more than just the number of spins we thought were possible. He had shown us a grace and ease that we did not know how to measure and, thus, did not know how to achieve. And he knew he had done something special. He would not ride again that day. He leaned his bike against the wall of the café and became the center of the crowd still willing to watch the rest of us. We went again and again up the hill to ride down and spin through the intersection. Hardly anyone fell. We all knew we were having fun, but we—all of us, even Jerry McCloskey—rode without heart.

The effect of Bradshaw Morgan's ride went beyond that day. It marked the end of a season. We still rode, but we climbed the hill less often and without Bradshaw. Without saying anything about it, we waited for spring. Our parents talked about closing the venetian blind business. March came. One Saturday, some men loaded the drills and saws and other tools belonging to our father's business onto a truck, and a deputy sheriff padlocked the doors. Our father spent the whole weekend sitting in his chair in the living room and staring at something beyond the window. On Monday morning, he left before we were ready for school, and Momma told us he had a new job as a salesman in a furniture store in Terre Haute.

3

The snowfalls stopped, and the ice melted. On Saturdays, we rode four miles to the covered bridge over Raccoon Creek, and we planned how—later, when the dirt roads had dried out—we would go first to the bridge, then off the main road to the hogback. That was a ridge that ran for several miles parallel to the creek and formed steep bluffs along the bank that we climbed and sometimes jumped from into the water in the summer, but the water wouldn't be warm enough for that until June. In April, Momma told us our father had taken another job in a town called Sullivan, and we were moving when school was out. Nights in the apartment were quieter, and Will and I talked in the dark about the place called Sullivan. We agreed it had to be better than where we were, although we didn't know why it had to be. Sometimes when I stayed awake long enough, I heard a soft, soft sound like Momma trying not to cry.

Will and I collected empty boxes from the grocery store and stacked them on the landing and in the hall and put some in every room in the apartment. Momma packed our winter clothes and other things she knew we wouldn't need first. She made us help every evening after supper. We filled the empty boxes, stacked them in the hall and the kitchen, and went back to the grocery store for more. By the time our father came home a couple of days before the last day of school to help us finish packing, we were living around, in, and out of boxes. Momma looked tired, and there wasn't much finishing left to do when he got there. Then two days after school was out, two trucks drove up and parked on the street that ran next to the building.

They didn't come together. The first one there was a big stake-body job, with lettering on the cab that said APEX FURNITURE, SULLIVAN, IND. The driver was a little man with gaps between his teeth that showed a lot because he was always grinning. Our father called him Norman, and he called our father "Mr. Rambler" and "sir."

Norman wanted to start loading right away. Will and I were eager to help him, even though most of the boxes were too heavy for us to carry down the stairs and lift onto the back of the truck. He told

Norman to come upstairs and get some coffee. Will and I stayed down and climbed over the staked sides of the truck. We were figuring out how to walk all the way around the outside of the truck without getting on the ground when the second truck drove up. It was a van, all closed in with big double doors in the back. Estes Brothers, Auctioneers was painted in big black letters on the side of the van, and two men sat in the high cab.

The driver got out. He carried a clipboard with papers on it. He shouted, "Hey, kid. Is this where the Ramblers live?"

I said yes, and he started walking toward the front of the building. I called to him and pointed toward the double door–size opening for the stairs at the rear corner just as my father and Norman came through it onto the sidewalk.

The driver said, "Is one of you Mr. Rambler?"

He didn't say "Mister" in the respectful way Norman did.

My father said, "I am."

The driver looked at the opening, then at the windows on the second floor, and said, "Nobody told me this was a damned upstairs job."

Our father looked at Will and me and said, "Come down from there." When we were on the ground, he said, "I want you two to go play."

I said, "I want to help."

"There'll be plenty for you to help with later. This morning, I want you and Will to go play. Find some of your friends and set up a baseball game."

I started toward the stairs.

He said, "Where are you going?"

"To get my bike."

"No. Leave your bikes here."

I said, "What about Angie?"

"Go play!"

He looked like he wanted to say something else, but the two men with the second truck were already starting upstairs, and he turned and followed them.

Will said, "Come on." I went, but I didn't hurry.

We walked to the baseball field. A half dozen boys were already there hitting and chasing flies and grounders. Will and I didn't have gloves, so we went into the outfield and shagged the balls nobody could catch. After a while, there were enough for us to pick six on a side, with one left over. That one was Will because he was the youngest. I felt bad about him not playing, but he didn't seem to mind much. My side was picked to go in the field first, and by the time we got to come in to bat, Will had gone.

I remember very little about the game except what happened the next time I saw Will. I borrowed a glove from one of the guys at bat and played second base, which meant I faced the road. We had played at least three or four innings when I saw Will running toward the field. He was calling my name at the top of his voice. Everybody turned and watched him for a moment, until somebody got impatient and called us back to the game. The batter hit the ball on the ground toward me. I moved into position to field it, but a runner ran in front of me, and I lost sight of the ball. It went past me into the outfield, and everybody started yelling and screaming. Then I realized it was not a base runner who had blocked my view but Will, who had come onto the field. He was standing in front of me, and he was crying.

He yelled, "They're taking everything!"

I said, "What are you talking about?"

"They're taking everything away—even our bicycles. And that man and Daddy almost got in a fight because that man called our things a pile of junk!"

The others shouted at Will to get off the field. Somebody shouted at me to get Will out of the way and to get back into the game.

Will said, "Come on!" And I ran with him off the field.

Somebody yelled, "Don't come back!"

Once we hit the road, I ran ahead of Will. It was only four long blocks from the baseball field to the apartment. Nothing in town was more than seven or eight blocks from the apartment. Will called to me to wait for him, but I kept on running. When I got to where I could see the side of the building we lived in, my father, Norman, and the two men who came in the second truck were standing in the street behind the van with the rear double doors wide open. Momma and Angie stood together on the sidewalk. I ran around the front of the truck and stood on the edge of the sidewalk between Momma and the men on the street.

Momma said, "Come here, Mark."

I ignored her.

"Mark!"

I knew that tone and stepped back beside her. Her eyes were red, and she kept wiping at her nose with a wadded-up handkerchief. Angie had big streaks of tears on her cheeks. Will came up. He wasn't crying anymore. He squeezed in between Momma and me. The two men with the truck lifted the bicycles into the back of the van, closed the double doors, and pulled a heavy metal bar down across them. The driver handed his clipboard and a pencil to my father.

He said, "Sign there, at the bottom."

My father said, "Do you know when the auction will be?"

The driver said, "Have no idea."

My father signed, and the two men got into the truck. We all stood there and watched as the van turned the corner and disappeared. My father stood in the middle of the street, and I thought he looked almost as old as Grandpa Rambler did.

Norman said, "I'll back up to the door, so we can load the boxes."

Without going upstairs, I knew the men in the van had left the boxes we had packed. I knew that everything else was gone and that it was going somewhere to be auctioned. I knew that what was happening had something to do with my father's business failing, with him going bankrupt, with bills that didn't or couldn't get paid. I knew that was why he and Momma both looked old and tired—too tired even to argue. And I knew that was why Momma stood stiff and still when Father came up and put his arm around her shoulder like he was trying to shield her from a bitter wind. There wasn't any wind that day.

The truck Norman was backing up to the stairway backfired, and our father said, "We better get to work. It's a long way to go if we're going to get there before dark."

Momma said, "Everybody carries something, but don't try to carry anything too heavy for you."

Norman kept Will in the back of the truck with him, to help stack and arrange the boxes the rest of us carried down to them. We worked slowly at first. Momma and our father stopped every now and then and just looked at each other before one of them picked up another box and went down the stairs. But emptying one room seemed to make us eager to empty another, and we worked faster and faster.

We were nearly finished when a small crowd of kids, led by Jerry McCloskey, showed up at the corner. Most of them were on bikes, and they rode around, doing figure eights in the intersection. Ruth Ann Parker and Patsy Jukeman came to our side of the corner, and Angie went to meet them. They acted like girls and hugged one another and cried.

My father asked me, "Do you want to go tell anyone goodbye?"

I looked toward the corner. Jerry McCloskey was playing chicken with another kid Will's age and rammed his rear wheel.

I said, "No. Can Will and I ride in the back of the truck?"

He had planned for us to ride in the car with Momma and Angie. Norman said, "I'll ride with 'em."

That was enough. Our father drove the truck. Momma and Angie went ahead in the car so our father would know if they had trouble. When our father started the motor, the kids at the corner moved in front of the café. We turned and drove past them, and Jerry McCloskey and the other bigger kids on bikes rode into the middle of the street and followed us. Will sat with Norman on some boxes in the middle, but I found a small space where I could stand against the back stake-panel to watch the blurring motion of the road underneath me smooth out into a fine black line in the distance. The kids on their bikes spread across the road and pedaled hard. They had found a new game for the moment as they raced and maneuvered for position to lead the pack. The distance between them and the truck gradually increased, but the way my father drove the truck slowly through town kept them from falling very far behind.

I looked over their heads at the intersection and at Sweet's Hill rising beyond it. Both receded, getting smaller and smaller until the hill looked like a narrow strip of ribbon that hung straight down from the sky and stiffened when it met the pavement at the bottom. I thought for a moment that I could even see the figure of a lone rider at the top. I imagined it looked like Bradshaw, as though he were already waiting for the next winter's snow and ice. The truck went around a sharp curve, and Sweet's Hill vanished. At the edge of town, the riders who had followed us turned off and disappeared behind a fencerow overgrown with blackberry bushes. They were headed for the creek and the hogback. No one had waved or shouted.

Then there was nothing but the noise of dual tires on the blacktop and a broken white line in the center of the road, a line of diminishing dashes that pointed to some place we had lived in once. We were moving to a place called Sullivan. I had no idea where it was except that, by the sun, I knew we were headed south. We were moving because my father had gone bankrupt and because my mother sometimes cried in the night. We were moving because two men in a truck took away the things my parents called theirs and the bicycle that was the only thing I had ever called mine. No grown-ups had come to say goodbye to my parents. We had lived in Rossville less than two years, and that was not long enough for anyone to believe our coming or going was any great matter. We were moving on a warm, cloudless day with a sky the same color my bike had been on that Christmas morning. It had not been said, but we all knew we would soon move again. I told myself that that, too, would be no great matter.

I climbed carefully over the boxes to the front of the truck. I stood against the cab and let the warm wind strike me full in the face. The narrow strip of road and the tiny dashes of white down the middle widened and blurred beneath the front of the truck. Momma and Angie were well ahead of us so that whenever there was any kind of curve in the road, they were out of sight for a moment. The truck seemed to speed up when that happened. There was a small space where I could look through the back window of the cab and see my father. He hunched his shoulders like he was trying to push the truck toward whatever was ahead with his own weight. He drove with both hands hard on the wheel.

THE TICK IS FULL

MARK FELT THE tick even before he opened his eyes and saw it. Its head was buried in his thigh, and its body was dark and swollen, full of his blood. It had fallen from the elm tree onto the windowsill and then onto the bed jammed up against the window. There was no screen on the window. His father had promised to put up a new screen, but he didn't have time before he left to go out to Wichita to see about a new job. That was how the tick got in. Mark's problem was how to get it out. He sat up, looked at it, and thought about it sucking his blood. He pinched it gently and gave it a couple of tugs. He did not pull too hard because he did not want to break it off and leave its head buried in his leg. He was afraid of tick fever. He rested a minute and tried again. This time the tick just seemed to back out of its own accord. Mark threw it out the window at the barrel standing across the yard beyond the pump. When it hit the barrel, it made a sound like a soft rock.

Nature called. He grabbed his pants off the iron footrail of the bed and rolled them up. He moved slowly to keep from waking his brother, who still slept in the bed on the side away from the window. If he woke him, they would fight. That would wake his mother and sister, and his mother would come into the room and yell at them. She would stay and look at them until her eyes started getting wet and cloudy. Then she would turn away and leave the room, leaving behind her a wake of unspoken disappointment that he did not want to have to bear again. Not in the morning.

He eased out of the window, making sure there were no ticks on the sill, and dropped onto the grass. He wondered what time it was. The sun was on the other side of the house, but he knew the day was well started because the cloudless sky was so bright. He pulled on his pants and made a straight line for the path of planks that made a walkway to the privy. There were no ticks there, only spiders. Mr. Fields, the farmer they rented from, had warned him about the spiders in the privy. He had said to watch especially for black widows and, with an exaggerated laugh, added that he knew a man once who got bit on the end of his tallywhacker, and it swelled up to almost three times its normal size. Mark never knew whether to believe Mr. Fields or not, especially when he talked about how popular that man had been with the women for miles around until the swelling went down. When he used the privy, he kicked the boards in front of the hole because Mr. Fields had said that that would scare the spiders away.

He did not see any spiders that morning. On his way back to the house, he stopped at the pump, and with three or four motions of the handle, he started a stream of clear water that he caught in the cup hanging from the pump by a piece of baling wire. It was cold—the coldest water he had ever tasted from a well—and almost sweet. He lifted the pump handle again, gave it a slight nudge, and let it fall slowly of its own weight and momentum. He held both hands under the spout until the thin stream filled them, and then he splashed the water into his face. The shock brought him standing upright, sucking in breath.

He had turned to go back into the house when he heard the tractor coming fast. He liked the steady high whining sound the tractor made when it was in the road gear. He liked the way it sounded and felt, especially when he sat on the seat, high off the ground, in control of the most powerful machine he had ever seen. He heard the tractor gearing down in front of the house and then the big wheels crunching the rocks used to fill up ruts in the driveway. It backfired once, and then the engine noise stopped. Mark walked around the corner of the house just in time to see Mr. Fields climbing down from the tractor.

Mr. Fields said, "Morning, Mark-boy. Your momma up?"

Mr. Fields always called him that—Mark-boy—and it always sounded to Mark like the man was imitating somebody he had heard once in a movie or maybe on the radio.

Mark said, "Yes, sir."

Mr. Fields said, "Well, Mark-boy, you go tell her your daddy called, and he's gonna call back at nine."

Mark said, "Yes, sir. I'll tell her."

Mr. Fields said, "You come with her, Mark-boy. I got some things that need done around the yard. Some manure needs tossing out in the pasture."

Mark turned to run to the house and stopped. He heard, saw, or maybe only sensed something or someone, a movement no one else would have seen, and he knew that his sister, Angie, had been standing in the shadows behind the screen door and that she was already on her way to tell their mother the news.

Mr. Fields climbed back up the tractor and hit the starter. The explosion and then the roar of the tractor engine drove out any thought of an answer Mark might have made. Mr. Fields waved at him, backed the tractor onto the road, and drove off toward his house. Mark stood and listened to the buildup through the gears until the sound reached that high whine that leveled off and hung in the air like it was part of the boiling dust cloud thrown up by the big rear tires.

The back screen door slammed, and in a moment, he heard the pump handle working. He walked round the side of the house and found his mother at the pump. She was bent over the bucket she had just pumped full and was splashing water onto her face. She had a little towel on her shoulder, and she was still wearing only her nightgown. Her straight dark hair hung down past her shoulders in the back. Mark watched her a moment. He thought she probably was pretty, but he did not always like being made to recognize she was a woman. It especially bothered him when grown men—like Mr. Fields's son, Herschel—talked about how fine she was.

His mother dried her face and said, "Isn't it a beautiful day?"

He said, "Yes, ma'am."

She said, "Your daddy's gonna call."

"What do you think he wants?"

"I don't know, but I hope it's because he found a job."

"Does that mean we're going to move again?"

Something in his voice made her stop toweling herself and look at him.

"Probably," she said.

"To Wichita?"

"Wherever," she said.

Mark looked down at his feet. The conversation had taken a direction he did not want to follow. He did not like it where they were. He did not want to move again. He looked up at her.

He said, "Mr. Fields wants me to come with you. He has some work for me to do around the yard."

She stretched her arms out and up, reached back, and fluffed her hair. Her woman's shape pressed against the cloth of her gown, and Mark turned away toward the house.

She said, "You better eat something if you're going to work. There's some cereal. I think there's enough milk. Don't you and Angie fuss!"

He did not answer. In the kitchen, he took the milk bottle from the refrigerator. The glass felt cool. It was not cold. Nothing was ever kept *cold* in that refrigerator. He got a bowl and a box of dry cereal from the pantry. It was not really a pantry. It was a packing crate that had held a large piece of furniture. His father had brought it from town, stood it on end, put shelves in it, and called it a pantry. His mother had seemed pleased with it, but when Angie had laughed at it, his father had gone out and walked down the driveway into the darkness. He came back after everyone was in bed, but Mark was still awake and had heard his father and his mother talking in their bedroom. He had looked at the stars through his window, and now and then, he caught a word or two, especially *Wichita*; but mostly, he heard sounds like they were moving around a lot. He wished—he had been wishing every night—they could live in a house that had rooms farther apart and doors and windows that could be kept closed, and he would not have to hear what went on between his parents, especially at night.

Angie came into the kitchen and saw the nearly empty bottle of milk on the table.

She said, "You took it all?"

He said, "Momma told me to eat 'cause I have to go to work."

"Work where?"

"For Mr. Fields."

She said, "I know what you're going to have to do."

"What's that?" he said.

"Shovel shit," she said.

"Angie!"

Neither of them had noticed their mother come into the kitchen. She carried a bucket of water to the sink.

She said again, "Angie!"

"What!"

"Why do you talk like that?"

Angie said, "Because it's true. Yesterday afternoon, I saw Herschel pulling a wagonful of manure into the front pasture. You know for sure he isn't going to unload it, not when they've got Markie-boy here to do it."

She laughed. She was sixteen, three years older than Mark, and Mark thought he never could tell whether she merely despised him or intensely hated him, or why she acted as if she had become truly worried about him last winter when he had pneumonia. He thought that she was not quite pretty, and sometimes she smelled funny. He had shouted at her once to stay away from him until she took a bath, and his father took him for a long walk and tried to explain about girls' monthlies and how it was a terrible thing women had to put up with, and men had to learn to put up with it too. She wore shorts and a halter that was pulled up really tight. He thought it was to show she had breasts, even if they were small.

His mother said, "Mark, we have to hurry."

Angie said, "Markie-boy!"

"Stop it, Angie! Mark, get your shoes and wake up Will. Tell him to fill the barrel. Angie, when I get back, I want those dishes done. You were supposed to do that last night."

Angie said, "I am going with you."

"You're staying here. And I want you started on those dishes before I leave. Mark, hurry."

Mark went to the bedroom and shook Will. He pulled a T-shirt out of a drawer and pulled it on. He took the pair of socks he had worn the day before and had hung wrong-side-out over the back of a chair and put them on. His shoes were under the bed, one nearly to the wall.

He got them, put them on, and shook Will again. Will sat up in a sudden motion and swung at Mark, but Mark saw the swing coming and jumped back.

Mark said, "Momma said you got to fill the barrel."

Will said, "Why me?"

"I got to go to work at Mr. Fields's house."

"Doing what?"

"I don't know. Just make sure you put that barrel in the sun before you start to fill it."

"Why I gotta fill it?"

Mark said, "Momma said so, that's why. Now get up."

He picked up his Saint Louis Cardinals cap off the floor and put it on.

He said, "Put that barrel in the sun."

Outside, his mother yelled, "Mark!"

"Make sure that barrel's in the sun."

He ran out of the house. His mother was already walking out in the road. The road was gravel, and a fresh load of rock had been dumped on it only a few days earlier. They walked on the edge when they could, along the ditch; but most of the time, the edge of the ditch was either too steep or too full of milkweed and thistles. The sun was already up at a little more than a forty-five-degree angle. If Mr. Fields had been with them, he could have told them within a quarter hour what time it was.

Mark's mother walked in front. She had on a wide-brimmed straw hat to keep the sun off her head. She wore a thin summer dress that had tiny flowers all over it, and he could see all the straps of her woman's underclothes. She was thin, and she fought rather than stepped through the loose gravel. Her hair was pulled up under the hat, and small ribbons of dampness had already begun to form in the cloth of the dress on her back. Once, she stopped and pointed at the fence on the other side of the road. It was covered with blackberry vines heavy with nearly ripened fruit.

She said, "It's going to be time to pick berries soon."

Mark said, "Not if we move."

She looked back at him. He caught her look and held it for a moment. There was something in her eyes that unsettled him. She stumbled and looked forward again. Mark looked up at the sun and the sky and thought about Will getting up without anyone there except Angie to make him do his chores right. He bet that Will would move the barrel next to the pump to fill it. That would put the barrel in the shade of the elm nearly all day, and there would be no chance for the water to warm.

They turned into the driveway that led to a large frame house that sat nearly a hundred yards back from the road. The front pasture fence ran along the drive to within forty feet of the house. And Mark saw Angie was right.

The large flatbed trailer stood in the middle of the pasture. An irregular dark mound rose up from it, and he already knew how bad it was going to be, the sun already having worked on the manure for three or four hours. And that was just this morning. It had been out there since the day before. He could even see the thin handle of the fork sticking up out of the pile on the wagon.

Mr. Fields met them at the cattle guard that ran across the road where the front pasture ended and the house yard began. He held out a hand for Mark's mother to grab as she stepped carefully on the gapped pipes of the cattle guard. Mark wished he had thought of helping her. Mr. Fields took out a large pocket watch on the end of a leather fob and looked at it.

He said, "Nearly nine, ma'am. You better go on into the house. The wife is waiting for you. Probably in the kitchen. I'm going to get this boy started. Day's half gone, and there's a whole bunch of work has got to get done. Come see, Mark-boy."

Mr. Fields walked toward the front pasture. Mark watched his mother go toward the house. He had hoped to go with her, to be there when his father called. He ran to catch up with Mr. Fields.

"Herschel put a wagon of barn manure out in that pasture yesterday. Spread it all around, far as you can. You know how to do it."

Mark knew how to do it. He had done it before. The first time, he had tried to work too fast in order to get off the wagon as soon as he could. For days, his back hurt and his arms ached; and at night, his legs went into spasms that he thought would hurl him out of bed. He learned to pace himself after that. He took smaller loads on the fork, bent his knees the way his father had shown him, and used his legs to lift and throw. He thought it was the worst job on the farm, but somebody had to do it.

Herschel had said, "You doing it beats the hell outta me doing it."

On the wagon, Mark took the fork in his hands and began to lift and throw the manure. He was glad he had remembered to wear his cap. There was no shade, and the sun seemed to get larger as it climbed higher in the morning sky. He lifted and threw, trying to spread the loads around on the ground. He worked steadily and tried not to think about how his stomach felt about the smell and the green flies that flew all around him. He wondered about his mother and what his father was saying to her. He thought about Will and hoped he had put the barrel in the sun. He did not notice Herschel walking across the pasture toward the wagon.

Herschel said, "Spread that manure around good, boy."

The voice crept up the back of Mark's neck like the sound of a rake pulled across concrete. He turned and saw Herschel grinning at him. The grin on Herschel's face gave Mark another tremor of a chill.

Mark said, "I know how to spread it."

"Just checking on you, boy."

Herschel liked calling Mark *boy*. Mark thought Herschel liked bossing him and setting him up for the most unpleasant jobs, especially when Mr. Fields was not around. Mark thought Herschel spent a lot of time thinking of some kind of meanness to do to him.

Mark said, "Why you checking on me? Ain't you got your own work to do?"

"Don't get uppity now. A three-dollar-a-day hired kid don't have much room for getting uppity."

Mark looked at him a moment. Herschel was a short man, and he had gray eyes that never seemed to focus on anything. He was strong. Whenever there was a problem with an animal, including the Guernsey bull Mr. Fields rented for stud, Herschel handled it. Mark was a little bit afraid of Herschel, not so much of his strength as his strangeness. He was always talking about women other than his wife, and he pestered Angie every chance he had. And when he and Mark worked alone together in the barn, he talked about his parts and teased Mark, asking him if he had a man's parts yet. Mark turned away from the grin and the eyes that seemed to be looking somewhere else, picked up another load on his fork, and threw it.

Herschel said, "Hey, boy. You think your sister's a virgin?"

Mark said, "I don't know."

Herschel said, "How 'bout you, boy? You a virgin?"

Mark jammed the fork into the manure, and Herschel laughed. It was louder and deeper than Angie's laughter, but it had almost exactly the same mocking tone hers sometimes had.

Mark said, "What you laughing at?"

The laughter stopped, choked off, and Herschel's face was red. He took a dirty handkerchief out of his overalls and wiped his forehead with it.

Herschel said, "I'm laughing at you standing up there on that wagon pitching shit."

Mark put the fork into the soft, moist manure that was held together by pieces of hay, dirt, and feed. He lifted it up. He threw it out in the same general direction he had been throwing it before, but a little closer to Herschel. Herschel stepped back.

He said, "What the hell you doing, boy?"

Mark turned his back to Herschel and stuck the fork into the manure again.

Herschel said, "You better watch where you throw that manure, boy! You hit me with any of that, and I'll come up there and wash your face in it."

Mark picked up another load on the end of the fork. His back was still turned to Herschel, but he knew Herschel was watching him. He bent his knees and made a slight jerking motion to adjust his grip on the handle of the fork. Herschel backed up, tripped, and fell. Mark strained and threw the manure forward onto the ground on the side of the wagon opposite from Herschel. He stooped, picked up another load, and threw it forward again.

Herschel picked himself up off the ground and said, "Too bad you're moving, boy. I was hoping you'd stay around awhile. I figured I might get to hear your sister's cherry pop."

Mark did not turn around. He lifted another load of manure, but it was too heavy to throw. He shook some loose, threw the load, and stumbled a little. One foot jerked too far forward, and his shoe was covered with brown and green muck. *Moving.* Now he knew why his daddy had called. *They were.* He did not notice Herschel leave. He had known it probably would happen—*again.* He had heard his father and mother talking about it at night. Once he thought he had heard his mother crying. He could not be sure that was what he heard, but much later that night, he was still awake, looking at the stars through the holes in the elm and hearing it again. It was like the sound of the wind that stirred the leaves of the elm, but softer.

Women's voices came from the house yard. Mark saw his mother and Mrs. Fields standing outside. His mother walked away a few steps, turned back, and spoke to Mr. Fields. She walked away and turned back again. He watched her. She was too far away for him to talk to her. He wanted to know what his father had said. He thought of Herschel learning before he did what his father's message had been, and he jammed the fork down too hard and stuck it in the wood bed of the wagon. He worked it loose and began again to lift and throw. He glanced between each load to see where his mother was until she disappeared where the blackberry vines were the thickest along the fence.

He worked faster, and with each forkful, he measured what he had left to do. He wanted to go home. He wanted to hear his mother talk about what his father had said. He jabbed, lifted, and threw. Sweat ran down from under the band of his cap, and he wiped at it with his arm. The sun moved higher and was nearly straight overhead when he heard the tractor. He turned and saw Mr. Fields driving toward him. He scanned what was left on the wagon, looked up at the sun, and knew it was lunchtime. He needed ten minutes.

Mr. Fields drove the tractor to the side of the wagon and sat with the motor running. He watched Mark. He waited until Mark threw the last fork of manure onto the ground.

Mr. Fields shouted, "It's lunchtime, Mark-boy."

Mark nodded against the roar of the tractor, laid his fork down on the wagon bed, and stepped onto the frame of the tractor. He stepped up to a narrow place beside Mr. Fields and held on to the seat as Mr. Fields put the tractor in gear and eased it forward. He drove slowly into the barnyard and let Mark off at the water trough in the empty pen nearest the house. Mark understood, and he turned the valve on the spigot over the trough. He put his head under the flow of water coming from the pipe. The water was not as cold as the water he had pumped from the well at his house, but it cooled him. He let it flow over his arms and hands. He turned, just in time to see Herschel coming toward him and holding out a towel and a bar of homemade soap.

Mark thought Herschel meant to hurt him because the manure had come so close to his feet when Mark threw it. Mark knew that Herschel could hurt him. He was Mr. Fields's son, but he was full-grown, larger than his daddy was.

Herschel said, "Full of shit, ain't you, boy?"

Mark took the soap and rubbed it in his hands and up and down his arms. It was rough and stung the inside of his arms, but it got him clean enough to go to the table and eat without smelling the manure he had been tossing.

Herschel said, "I put your towel on the trough. Hurry up."

A huge sycamore shaded the front corner of the house. Under the tree, there was a wooden table with two benches streaked with dirty gray scabs that had once been white paint. Mark's plate and a glass of milk were already on the table with a knife and fork wrapped in a cloth napkin. He ate roast pork, potatoes, gravy, slaw, peas—more than he could hold comfortably. He had hardly finished when Mr. Fields and Herschel came out the kitchen door and walked toward him. Mr. Fields sat across from him, and Herschel slid in next to Mark on the bench.

Mark started to slide toward the other end, but Herschel grabbed his arm and held him in front of his plate.

Mr. Fields said, "Had enough, Mark-boy?"

"Yes, sir."

Mark turned to get off the bench, but Herschel's hand clamped on the fleshy part of Mark's thigh, right where the tick had been. Mark squirmed and looked down at his plate. He felt tears coming into his eyes, and he knew that Herschel was grinning. It was a game Herschel liked to play. Mark dropped his fork onto his plate, and Herschel let go. Mark looked up and wondered whether or not Mr. Fields knew what was happening under the table. Herschel's hand stroked Mark's thigh twice then patted it, and Mark squirmed away from him.

Mr. Fields said, "Herschel told you your daddy said you're moving?"

Mark said, "Yes, sir. To Wichita."

Herschel said, "Where the hell is Wichita, boy?"

Mark knew where it was. After the third or fourth night that he heard his father and mother talking about it, he looked it up on an old US road map his father had brought home. It was a long way from Indiana, across Illinois and Missouri. It was going to be a long ride, even if Illinois was a narrow state on the map.

Mark said, "In Kansas."

Mr. Fields said, "Your momma said he's got himself a real good job in an airplane factory."

Herschel said, "How come your daddy don't ever stay with nothin'? How long you think you'll be in Wichita before you move again?"

Mr. Fields said, "Leave him alone, Herschel. What his daddy does isn't your business."

Mark slid off the bench, picked up his plate and utensils, and carried them to the little stoop at the kitchen door. His thigh hurt him. He could still smell the manure in his nostrils, and he wanted to go home to help his mother pack. He turned from the stoop and collided with Mr. Fields. Mr. Fields grabbed Mark's hand and pushed a crumpled bill into it. It was a five. He usually paid him only three dollars and never before the day was over.

Mr. Fields said, "You better go on home. Your momma needs some help. Tell her I'll be around later to see if she needs anything from town."

Mark mumbled thanks, shoved the money into his pocket, and started for the front pasture. When he was with his mother, he used the driveway and the road; but when he was by himself, he cut diagonally across the front pasture and climbed the fence. He was already thinking about what he had been told and wondered how they could possibly move tomorrow. He pictured the map and the highway that wound toward Wichita, and he knew that even if his daddy drove all night, he could not get home in time to leave *tomorrow*. He walked along the fence until he was well past the line that would have taken him near the wagon and the spread manure, and he turned toward the farthest corner. He was a little more than halfway when he heard the sound of the smaller tractor—Herschel's tractor—coming behind him. He did not look around. He broke into a run for the fence, but he was not quick enough. The tractor, with Herschel sitting on top of it, pulled in between Mark and the fence. Herschel was grinning.

Mark said, "What you want?"

Herschel said, "I want you to do something for me."

"What?"

Herschel took a folded piece of paper out of his shirt pocket and leaned down to hand it to Mark.

Mark said, "What's that?"

Herschel said, "Take it. Take it, boy. It ain't nothing gonna hurt you."

Mark reached up and took the paper from Herschel's hand. He started to unfold it.

Herschel said, "Uh-uh, it ain't for you. That's for your sister. You take that to Angie, and don't you read it. You read it, I'm gonna find out about it. I'll take meat out of your leg next time."

Mark said, "What's this for?"

"Never mind. Just take it to her, but don't you let nobody else see you giving it to her. And I promise, I'll know if you don't give it to her just like I said."

Herschel pulled himself back up straight on the seat of the tractor and released the clutch. The tractor jumped forward. Mark felt the movement of air caused by the tire almost taller than he was rolling inches in front of him. The tractor was just past him, and he took off on a run for the fence. The blackberry vines tore his shirt, and the barbed wire scratched a hand. He got over the fence, jumped the ditch, and tried to run in the new loose gravel. He fell twice, picked himself up, and moved to the side of the road, where it was easier. Running, he didn't notice the milkweed and thistles.

He stopped to catch his breath and realized he still held the piece of paper Herschel had given him. He unfolded it, and at that moment, he knew that Herschel's threats had guaranteed his reading the note—that he would have crawled through fire and a whole army of South American soldier ants that eat everything in their way just to read the note. It said,

Angie,

Tonight after your lights go out. The old barn.

—H.

Rage flooded over him. *H*! It was as though Angie would know who that was, as though she had been familiar with him before. He stood on the edge of the road and looked up at the afternoon sun, a large white ball of fire that seemed nearly a match to what was happening inside of him. Tears of fury streaked his cheeks. His thigh—where the tick had drained his blood and where Herschel had squeezed it—hurt him. The smell of manure mixed with dirt and straw and covered with green flies came rushing back at him. And above all of it, he saw Angie running across a thin wisp of cloud in the pale blue sky with Herschel—large, powerful like the tractor—chasing her toward the dark purple of a distant thunderstorm.

"Mark! Mark!"

It was his mother's voice. She stood in the road by the mailbox. He shoved the note into his pocket and ran through the loose gravel of the road toward her.

She said, "How come you're not working?"

He said, "I finished spreading most of the manure, and Mr. Fields said you needed help. He said we're leaving tomorrow."

"That's right."

"How can we do that? Daddy can't get back from Wichita that fast."

"He's not in Wichita. He called from Saint Louis. He'll be home tonight, if he doesn't have any more car trouble."

They walked toward the house. *Tonight.* He saw the barrel standing next to the pump in the shade.

He said, "Look at that! Will put the barrel in the shade."

His mother said, "I'm sorry. With everything on my mind, I just didn't pay any attention to what he had done. I'll get you some clothes. Looks like you need shoes too. Just drop those dirty ones in the bucket by the steps when you finish."

Mark looked at the barrel. Will had filled it to within inches of the top, and that meant the water at the bottom was cold enough to take away one's breath, cold enough to make lips turn blue. Even if it had sat all day in the sun, the bottom would be cold. But now, after sitting only a few hours and in the shade, there would be no part, no depth, that would be bearable. The kitchen door slammed shut, and Will came toward him carrying clothes and a towel and soap—the same kind of harsh soap that Herschel had brought to the trough. Will came within a few steps of Mark, dropped the bundle, and ran back to the house yelling "Momma!"

Mark shouted, "You better run!"

He stripped and threw his dirty clothes in a pile. Taking a bath was awkward. The upright barrel was too tall to step into, and he wanted to hurry. He picked up the soap and lifted himself up and into the barrel and let himself down slowly into the water. The cold exploded through his body. He felt his scrotum shrivel. The water came up almost to his armpits, and he tried to fight against the consciousness of the pain by jumping up and down. He rubbed himself with the soap as quickly as he could, submerged once, pulled himself up, and jumped out onto the ground. His flesh looked like a fresh-plucked chicken's. He heard somebody giggle and turned around only to see nothing more than movement behind the screen door. It was Angie. He kept himself covered in the front with one end of the towel and wiped at the rest of his body with the other end. He was not dry, but he dressed anyway, picked up his dirty clothes, and remembered the note. He fished it out of a pocket, dropped the dirty clothes into the bucket beside the back step, and ran to the privy. He pulled the door shut behind him and threw the note into the hole.

Angie was in the kitchen taking things out of the cabinets and putting them on the counter and table. Mark found his mother in her bedroom. Her bed was covered with clothes. Drawers were pulled out, and a half dozen empty boxes took up most of the bare space on the floor. His mother looked tired. She folded clothes slowly and laid them on the bed in stacks, as though the decision of what else to do with them was, at that time, more than she could handle. Mark promised himself he would spend whatever time it took to help her get ready for moving.

She said, "Help Angie in the kitchen. And leave Will alone. I got enough to do without having you two start up."

When Mark returned to the kitchen, Will jumped toward one end of the long table that filled the center of the room. Mark ignored him and watched Angie stuffing newspaper in glasses and placing them in boxes. He thought Angie's eyes looked strangely red and puffy.

He said, "What's the matter?"

Angie said, "Nothing. Here, you do this. Do the glasses first, then the other dishes. Be careful. Pack them tight."

"You've been crying."

"Mind your own business. *Here.* This oughta be easier than shoveling cow dung."

She handed him a glass and a piece of newspaper. He took them and looked at her. She had a bright-yellow barrette in her hair, but she wore no makeup. He watched her, and he knew he had done the right thing with the note. He thought that she may not be very pretty, but she was too, too fine for somebody like Herschel Fields. He finished wrapping the glasses she had put out on the table and looked about for something else to do.

Angie said, "Daddy found a house."

Mark said, "I hope it has a bathtub inside."

Angie said, "I just hope it's in town and not stuck twenty miles from nothin' in the country."

They worked steadily the rest of the afternoon. Their mother moved about packing, directing them, giving them new jobs as they were about to finish others. Mark worked and watched Angie. Most of the time, they worked well together. Once, Mark tripped, juggled the bowl he was carrying to her, stumbled forward, caught his balance, and set the bowl on the table. Angie laughed. It made Mark feel good because it was not mocking or taunting laughter. He laughed too. Then he picked up the bowl and acted as though he would go through the routine again, pretending to stumble. They both laughed, and Mark had to set the bowl down to keep from dropping it. They had to stop working, and they laughed only because they were tired and because they were laughing together.

Mark put out his hand as though to keep from falling, and his hand landed on Angie's shoulder. Angie pushed him away, stopped laughing, and began packing dishes again—all, it seemed to Mark, in more or less the same motion.

Mark was outside getting water at the pump when Mr. Fields drove into the driveway in his pickup truck. was still light, but the sun had fallen behind the row of trees that hid the old barn from the house. Mark went to meet him.

Mr. Fields said, "Your daddy called again, Mark-boy. He's not gonna get here till real late, maybe not till after midnight. His water pump busted in Effingham. Tell your momma I'll come back in the morning to settle up everything."

Mark said, "Where's Effingham?"

Mr. Fields said, "Somewhere in Illinois."

Mark thought of the shape of Illinois on the map and tried to picture in his mind just where his daddy might be with a busted water pump.

Mr. Fields said, "You're a fine boy, Mark. I wish you were staying."

Mark said, "Yes, sir." That was because he did not know what else to say.

Mr. Fields backed the truck down the driveway, and Mark waited until it was in the road before he ran to the house. He told the others what Mr. Fields had said. They all continued to work, but what had been plain fatigue quickly became complete exhaustion. They worked and watched the clock on top of the refrigerator. They strained to make the time pass more quickly.

Finally, their mother said, "That's it. Enough. We'll finish in the morning."

Angie and Mark protested, but not strongly. Their mother promised to wake them if they were sleeping when their father came home. They discovered that Will had already given up and was unconscious in his bed. Mark climbed over Will and lay against the wall. He brushed off the windowsill, and through the holes in the elm, he watched the stars. There were two very close together, and he imagined they were himself and Angie, twinkling and moving across the cloudless dark sky.

A dog barked somewhere and another answered. Then the second one barked again, and Mark recognized it. It was Herschel's small mongrel that yapped in a high, whiny voice and ran away if anyone ever turned at him and said boo. He watched the moon, a three-quarter ball of light with shadows made to dance by the elm leaves moving only slightly in the air, and he heard the yap again. It was closer, from the wrong direction, and Mark knew that Herschel was going to the old barn to wait for Angie. He held his breath and listened. The dog yapped and stopped so suddenly, as though it had been cut off in midyap, and nothing else made a sound except the crickets. Herschel was waiting.

Mark grabbed his pants, leaned over the foot of the bed, and found his shoes. He eased out of the window, dropped to the grass, and stooped against the side of the house and listened. Nobody stirred. He pulled on his pants and put on his shoes without any socks and went down the line of planks and past the privy. The grass in the field was wet with heavy dew. He headed straight for the tree line to the west, where the sun had gone down and where the moon was already aiming. The three-quarter ball hung in the sky and, with the stars, made it easy for him to find his way. When he came to the tree line, he stopped and caught his breath. From the darkest shadows of the trees, he saw the old barn not more than thirty yards away.

The old barn looked frozen, a shape of light and dark grays, lines that ran into and met somewhere in shadows that seemed to hold their breaths. Nothing moved. The stars and the moon gave off a light that gave him a slight chill even though the night air was still and full of heat. An owl hooted in the woods a hundred yards or more on the other side of the old barn, and there was movement in the shadows farthest to his left. Herschel's mongrel ran into the light and came straight for him, found him, and began circling and yapping. Mark tried to move around a tree into even deeper shadow, but the dog shifted with him. It was smart enough to stay just out of reach of Mark's foot. The heavy door of the barn creaked open, and Mark saw Herschel coming toward him. He ran to the next tree.

Herschel said, "Don't run. I've got something good for you."

Mark retreated to another tree.

Herschel said, "Come on out, Angie. You know you want it. That's why you came out here."

Mark turned and ran, tripped, fell, got up, and ran again until he realized that he was out of the shadows and in the light. He stopped and turned back toward where he heard Herschel running. Herschel stopped too. He stepped out of the shadows and took a couple of steps toward Mark until he realized it was not Angie who had come to meet him.

Herschel said, "What the hell are you doing here?"

Mark backed up a couple of steps. Herschel matched his movement forward.

Mark said, "I came to tell you you're not doin' anything to my sister."

Herschel stared at him and then threw his head back and laughed. It was the strangest laugh Mark had ever heard. His legs were suddenly weak.

Herschel stopped laughing and said, "Okay, Markie-boy. You want it instead, that's okay. Hell yeah."

Herschel lunged at Mark, but Mark was quicker. The lunge made Herschel lose his balance, and he fell sprawled on the ground. Mark ran. He did not know where he was running to. He went around the old barn. His own blood pounded in his ears, and his breath came in gasps that sounded like small screams. He heard Herschel coming up behind him, heavy-footed, muttering curses. The little dog ran after him, circled him, snapped at his heels, ran back to Herschel, and caught up again with Mark, yapping all the time. Mark crossed the one wooden fence remaining behind the old barn and ran for the woods. He looked back and saw Herschel coming over the fence and then veering off to his right. Mark had made a mistake. He had forgotten the ditch and the barbed wire fence that ran along the edge of the woods. There was only one place he could cross the ditch, and Herschel had, in a few steps, cut him off from it. He stopped. Herschel stopped, and they faced each other.

Herschel said, "Got you now, Markie-boy. Your ass is mine."

There were still twenty yards between them, and Mark turned and ran back toward the barn. Mark reached the fence and was up on the first rail with the little dog scooting under him and yapping and jumping at him. Then he heard the sounds of boards cracking and splintering, and Herschel yelled. The dog jumped high and turned in the air, and before its feet touched ground, it was running toward where Herschel had cried out. Mark looked and could not see Herschel. The little dog ran in a ten- or twelve-foot circle, yapping at the ground. Mark let himself down from the fence and walked toward the place where the dog was circling. He saw the broken boards first, a row of rotted planks set side by side to cover a hole. Herschel's heavy step had been too much for the boards. They were brittle from the rain and sun bleaching and rotting them out. Then he smelled the stink. Herschel had fallen into an old privy hole that had never been completely filled up, probably left there when the barn was abandoned. The little dog jumped on Mark, not snapping now. It was just jumping and running around, yapping at the opening where Herschel had disappeared.

Then came a sound—a low, soft moan coming from the hole. The dog went into a frenzy. It yapped and leaned so far forward that Mark thought it would fall into the hole. He heard the sound again, louder, and the moan turned into a roar.

"Get me out of here. Help me!"

Mark moved to the edge of the hole and looked down. He saw something move—something large, deep in the darkness of the hole. He heard it splashing in the water.

"Get me out of here. There's things down here. They're crawling on me. Get me out of here. Markie! Markie! Help me!"

Mark yelled, "You're gonna hurt me."

"No! I promise. Get me out. I'm drowning in shit! Come on, boy!"

"What can I do?"

"Beside the barn, they's some fence posts that wasn't ever used. Get the longest one and bring it here. And hurry up."

Mark climbed the fence and looked alongside the barn. He almost missed them, but there were a half dozen or so long posts lying in the weeds next to the building. Mark pulled three or four of them out, took the longest one, and dragged it back to the hole. The dog still yapped, and Herschel was making slapping sounds.

When Mark looked over the edge again, Herschel yelled, "What's keeping you, boy? They's leeches down here sucking my blood in all this shit. Oh damn!"

Mark said, "What do I do?"

Herschel said, "Put one end down here. Easy. Hold on to that other end. Don't let it fall on my head."

Mark lowered the post into the hole. It was hardly halfway in when he felt Herschel's strength pulling on it.

Herschel said, "Don't let go dammit."

Herschel wedged one end of the post into the side of the hole. Mark felt Herschel's weight almost tear the post out of his hands. He dug his heels into the ground and hung on. In a moment, Herschel's head and shoulders appeared above the ground, and Mark wanted to run. Herschel must have realized Mark's fear because he screamed, "Don't let go!"

Herschel pulled himself up onto the edge of the hole, and Mark felt the release of the man's weight from the other end. Mark turned the pole loose and ran to the fence, climbed over it, and hid in the shadow of the barn. He watched Herschel moving around, almost like he was doing a little dance, slapping at himself until he suddenly started taking off his clothes. Mark learned that Herschel did not wear underwear. When he took off his overalls and his shirt and his shoes and socks, he was left standing naked in the pale, washed-out light of the waning moon. He pulled at things on his body and threw them on the ground.

Herschel said, "Leeches!"

Suddenly, Herschel kicked his clothes into the hole and walked away across the field toward the gravel road. Mark thought he limped. The little dog ran ahead of him and back to circle his heels and ahead of him again. Mark watched them until Herschel became a dark, indistinct figure in the distance. Mark thought he could tell when Herschel reached the fence that ran beside the gravel road, and then Herschel disappeared.

Mark walked back to the house. He walked around the house to make certain no one was awake. He stopped by Angie's window and looked in. She lay on her bed uncovered. She wore a pale cotton nightgown. Her hair lay loose and spread out on her pillow. She turned toward him, moved as though to stretch, and then curled up her knees almost up to her chest. She breathed easily. Her body rose and fell in a slow rhythmic motion, and Mark caught his breathing matching her rhythm. He watched her only a few minutes. Afraid she might wake and see him, he moved away from the window. The moon was gone and few stars remained. Rapidly moving heavy clouds darkened the sky. Mark had no idea what time it was, but he knew he was not going back to bed.

Through the field on Angie's side of the house, he could reach the path that ran alongside the road up the small hill to where he could see the headlights of cars traveling the paved highway. He walked easily, looking now and then up at the sky and wondering if it was going to rain. Mr. Fields had told him a real farmer could smell the rain before it came. Mark couldn't smell anything different. At the top of the hill, he sat and leaned against a fence post and waited. To his left, the hill sloped easily back toward the house, where his mother and Will and Angie slept safely. He could see the tree line beyond the house, but the barn was out of sight.

He looked at the dark outline of the house and thought of Angie lying in her bed, sleeping, breathing easily with her knees tucked up under her chin. Every now and then, he saw again the ugliness of Herschel's face and heard the heavy-footed sound of Herschel running after him, but all that disappeared when he saw the headlights turn off the highway onto the gravel road.

He jumped up and ran onto the road. He had forgotten about the tick that stole his blood, the weight of the fork loaded with manure pulling on his back and arms, the fear that had kept him running when Herschel was close behind, and the smell of the hole Herschel had fallen into. He was already thinking about the days ahead with no more Herschel and with Angie safe and all of them moving to Wichita. He had never been happier in his life than he was right then, standing in the middle of the road with his arms over his head, flailing wildly in rhythm with his heart.

ALL IN A DAY'S WORK

I SPENT THE afternoon re-sorting boxes of shoes on the shelves in the stockroom of Stricter's Discount Fashion Shoe Store. While I worked, I listened to some guy with a really creamy voice on the radio. He was getting bent out of shape because it was Friday afternoon. He couldn't breathe without saying "TGIF." I figured that he didn't have to work on Saturdays.

Garland Weed, the assistant manager, stuck his head into the aisle of shelves where I was working and said, "Customers!"

I said, "Where's Stricter?"

"He's out. Get your ass in gear. You've got customers."

That meant one of two things: either we had a sudden rush of business at almost closing time on Friday afternoon (which wasn't likely), or someone Garland didn't want to wait on had come in (which was most likely). I tapped the last box into place and followed him. There were no customers in the showroom. Garland was standing at the front door, rocking back and forth on his heels and watching something going on outside.

I said, "Where are the customers?"

He said, "Look there." And he laughed.

I went over, stood beside him, and looked through the glass door. Two women stood on the curb on our side of the street and looked back toward the other side. They were yelling at another woman trying to cross the street to come meet them. The one trying to cross the street was tall, and her hair was a stringy blond. She acted drunk. Traffic was pretty heavy right then, and three or four times, she looked like she might walk or spin or fall right into a moving car. Once she started to go back to the other side, but the two on our side of the street yelled at her and got her to turn around again. She finally made it to the curb and fell laughing into the arms of the other two. They held her up, and the three of them came toward the store. Garland and I both moved away from the door toward the back of the showroom.

The women were whores. They practiced their craft and art across the street, upstairs over a hardware store, in a place called Pleasure Palace Rooms. They sometimes came to the store late on Friday afternoons when they knew the Saturday sale tables would be out. Garland used to try to wait on them, but after he found out they probably weren't ever going to buy much of anything we had for sale and they weren't giving any free samples of what they had for sale, he passed them on to me—like I needed something else to occupy my Friday afternoons, or like I needed to shoot myself in the foot.

My father and the three whores walked in together. My father even held the door open for them. I hadn't seen him coming. He must have been parking his car while Garland and I were watching the women carry on out in front, and he just happened to walk up at the same time the whores arrived at our door. Someone told me once that luck is just a matter of timing. The three women headed for the sale tables, and my father walked along the side toward the back.

The blonde looked back at Garland and me and said, "Hi, Mark. We came to see what you got on the table."

"Hi, Mark!" She said it like we were old friends, with my father smiling as he stood on the side in the Children's Shoes section. Her name was Mary Ann. I knew her because she was the one who came the most often to check out the stuff on the sale table, and she never bought anything. I had always thought she was kind of pretty for what I thought whores were supposed to look like.

I said, "Look all you want." But I didn't call her by name. I went to greet my father. He had moved over to the Tennis and Running section.

He said, "I can wait. Take care of your customers."

Garland came over and said, "Go ahead, Mark. I'll keep your father company."

Usually, Mary Ann and one or two others came into the store, picked over the shoes on the sale table enough to make me have to straighten them out, and left. Maybe once a month, one of them bought something. The first time or two they came after I started working there, I must have acted like they bothered me because the next day, Stricter said things like "Whores need shoes." And once, he had said, "Hath not a whore feet?" I got used to them, and they never caused any problems other than wasting my time.

Mary Ann tripped over one of the little stools I sat on to fit shoes on a customer. She stumbled a couple of times and had to grab the back of a chair to catch her balance.

She said, "Where'd that goddamned thing come from?"

I shoved the stool under a chair and out of the way. The other two stopped looking at shoes and turned toward Mary Ann. I hadn't seen either of the other two before. One was a brunette; I thought she was probably at least thirty years old. She looked like she might have been pretty when she was younger. The other one had brown hair that looked like it needed combing. I couldn't tell how old she was, but she was clearly the oldest, maybe older than my mother. I didn't know whores did what they do when they were that old.

The brunette said, "I told you she's too damned drunk. We shouldn't've brought her."

Mary Ann said, "You go to hell. I'm not too drunk. If I'm too drunk, I'll go to hell with you."

I glanced back at my father and Garland. I couldn't tell what they might be thinking. Garland grinned.

The oldest one held up a pair of ugly sandals and told Mary Ann, "These are your size. Why don't you try them on? The kid'll help you."

I hated being called kid, but I ignored it. I pointed at the clock on the wall behind the cash register and said, "Have you found anything you'd like to try on? We close in less than ten minutes."

The brunette held up three different shoes and said, "I want to try these."

She handed me the shoes she wanted to try and sat in one of the chairs, and I pulled out a stool and sat in front of her. I took one of her old shoes off her foot and put one of the new ones on—a red sandal with straps that tied high above the ankle. No problem. She sat like any proper lady.

Mary Ann went back to one of the tables and started throwing shoes around.

She shouted, "Where are those red sandals?"

I said, "What size?"

She said, "Seven."

I said, "Maybe you mean these."

She looked at the sandal on the brunette's foot and said to no one or to everyone, "I'd expect that bitch to take my shoe."

The oldest one said, "Stop talking like that."

The brunette reached down, undid the sandal, and handed it back to me. Mary Ann came over and sat in the chair next to the brunette, pulled up her skirt over her knees, and stuck a foot up toward me.

"Try it on," she said.

She gave me her foot and showed me everything. And I mean everything because she wasn't wearing anything under her skirt. I discovered immediately that she was not a natural blonde.

Stricter had warned me that that kind of thing happens sometimes in the life of a shoe salesman. All I needed to do was be cool and never let on that I had noticed it. It had happened to me before. I believe Garland hoped it would happen with every woman he waited on. He kept score. He'd run through the curtain into the backroom and shout, "Beaver! Beaver!" This time I wished it was him sitting on that stool, looking up a drunk whore's leg at the mystery of the universe. That's what Stricter called it.

I put the red sandal on her foot, wrapped the straps around her ankle, and tied them. She got up, walked around, and stood in front of a mirror over by my father and Garland. She sort of pushed herself between them and turned to my father.

"Like it?"

My father smiled and acted like he was paying a lot of attention to her foot before he said, "It's you."

Mary Ann laughed then said, "Are you his daddy?"

"Yes."

"He's cute."

I sat on the stool and wished I could crawl under the carpet. Mary Ann went to the table, got the mate to the sandal, and brought it to me.

She said, "I'll take them. I'll wear them." And she sat in the chair, lifted her foot, and gave me the grand view again.

The brunette said, "For Christ's sake, why don't you sit right?"

Mary Ann said, "I think she's jealous."

I hurried and put the other sandal on Mary Ann's foot and put her foot down on the floor. I was starting up from the stool when Mary Ann leaned over and said in a whisper meant to be too loud, "Save that black-haired bitch over there for when you're already loaded up on penicillin."

The brunette charged at Mary Ann and got both hands in her blond hair. She pulled Mary Ann out of the chair just as Stricter walked in.

Stricter bellowed, "What's going on here?"

Neither Mary Ann nor the brunette paid any attention to him. Between them, it was like sixteen variations of fury broke loose all at once. They used fists, although it didn't look like many blows really landed very sharply. They grabbed hair, scratched, fell onto and off chairs, got up, and went at each other, pushing and pulling and swinging and kicking and yelling names at each other. I doubt if I could remember half the names they called each other, but I sure heard a lot of imaginative suggestions about what they could do to and with various parts of their anatomies.

Stricter yelled, "Garland, call the police."

I expected Stricter to grab hold of them or to do something to stop them, but he just sort of circled around them, not getting close enough to get caught by a flailing fist or a flying foot.

Garland moved toward the display case where the telephone was, but he didn't pick it up to call anyone. I decided I had to do something. Why? Because they were my customers? Because I wanted to impress my father? Stricter? Because I was just dumb?

They stopped, as though they were each taking a moment to catch their breath. They faced each other, and I stepped between them.

I said, "That's enough."

I faced the brunette. I don't know why I faced the brunette instead of Mary Ann. I just did.

"I said that's enough!"

I felt Mary Ann moving behind me, and I turned just my head to see what she was doing. She was just moving aside and half-straightening her clothes. I looked at Mary Ann long enough that I didn't see the brunette take one step back and two to the side. I turned back toward her, just in time to see the strain of effort in her face and the blur of her leg as her pointed shoe came up and caught me exactly in the middle between my two big toes. I went down. I thought I would throw up on the carpet. I rolled over, held myself, and made strange noises. An incredible pain started between my legs and attacked the back of my head. The pressure of somebody's hands kept me from rolling around, and in a moment, the sharp nausea and pain became a dull wave washing over me.

The pressure was from my father holding me down, putting his hand in my belt, pulling up, and telling me to suck in air. Stricter got the whores out of the store while I was down. I heard yelling and cursing, but I didn't really know what was going on. My father helped me up into a chair. Garland was still behind the display case. Stricter said, "I'll help Garland with the closing, Mark. You sit there for a while."

My father said, "When you feel like it, I'll buy you supper."

I said, "I'm not hungry."

I sat there with a numb pain and an unsettled stomach while Stricter and Garland went through the routine of closing the store. Maybe twenty minutes later, I was standing on the sidewalk in front, looking across at the lighted windows above the hardware store.

My father said, "Did anyone else realize that the blonde walked off in her new shoes without paying for them?"

I turned on him and waited for him or Stricter to say something about what I should have done about it.

Stricter said, "I guess I didn't pay attention in all the commotion. I hate to lose merchandise that way, but I'll be damned if I'm going up there to get them."

Do not ask me why I did what I did next. I don't know if it was because I thought they were laughing at me or if they had just reminded me of something happening that made me mad or if I suddenly wanted to prove I wasn't going to let any whore get the best of me. I don't know why I did it, but I said, "Wait here." Then I ran across the street toward the stairwell. I heard my father shout at me to stop, then Stricter's voice calling my name, but I kept running until I was halfway up the stairs.

The only light on the stairs came from a small yellow bulb over the door at the top. The closer I got to the door at the top of the stairs, the more I thought I even had time not to do whatever I was going to do. I thought like that until I pushed the button on the wall beside the door, and from inside, I heard a chime and a rush of footsteps. Maybe there would have been time still to turn and go back down the stairs, but then there wasn't any time because the door opened, and a woman I had never seen before was standing in front of me. She was older than the three who had come to the store. She had gray hair and wore a long dress that hung straight from her shoulders to the floor.

She said, "What do you want?"

I said, "I want to see Mary Ann."

"How old are you?"

"Old enough."

I wondered if she could tell I was shaking inside.

"Are you sure you know what you're doing?"

I lied. "Of course." And I heard my voice too loud and too high. If I had tried to say anything else, my voice would have cracked the way it did when I was fourteen.

She smiled and stepped to one side to make room for me and then led me down a narrow hall. She opened a door for me, let me into a room, and closed the door behind me. I was alone in a room that had almost nothing in it except an old iron bed with one of those cheap-looking ribbed bedspreads that was faded from too many washings. A small throw rug lay next to one side of the bed. The linoleum floor and the rug looked washed out like the bedspread. The only light came from a table lamp on a nightstand by the head of the bed. It was a small lamp with a low-wattage bulb that gave off a soft light.

A door on one side of the room opened, and Mary Ann appeared. She was naked except for the red sandals with the straps wrapped high around her ankles. She carried a bowl of water in one hand and a bar of soap and a hand towel in the other.

She set the bowl on the nightstand and said, "Come here."

"What for?"

"Everybody gets washed first."

I looked at her, the first live naked woman I had ever seen. She had been transformed. I tried to look and not look at all of her all at once, but I couldn't do it. My eyes kept moving from part to part and stayed longer on some parts than on others. She was beautiful, and I stared. Even when I moved my eyes, I moved them from one stare to another. I hadn't known anybody that looked or could look like that. I had heard preachers invoke the holy wrath of hell on women like her, calling them tarnished and soiled, a menace to God-fearing men. No part of Mary Ann looked soiled or tarnished to me.

She sat on the edge of the bed, removed the red shoes, and placed them neatly on the hook rug.

She said, "Three dollars for a quickie. For five, you can have a little French."

I took a step toward her and said, "All I want is those shoes or five dollars."

She shouted, "What the hell are you talking about?"

"Those shoes. You didn't pay for them."

What happened next had to have happened like anything ever happens in time. Each little part had to happen after some other little part, and it all had to be in time because that's what time is—a number of little things happening all stretched out in a row. That's how time got invented by somebody doing something that led to another thing that led to something else; but right then, it didn't feel like what I was doing was happening in time. It didn't feel like anyone had invented time yet.

Mary Ann reached with both her hands for my belt buckle, but I surprised her and knelt and grabbed for the shoes with my left hand. I didn't surprise her enough because she moved, kicked one of the shoes under the bed, and stepped on my hand holding the other one. She wasn't hurting my hand, but I let go of the shoe when she pressed her naked leg against my shoulder, and the hair—the black hair of her triangle—scratched my face. I fell backward and jumped up.

She said, "You want your shoes back? Bring me my old ones. Now, before I start yelling for help, you better get out of here."

That's what I did. I went into the hallway, found the door that led outside, and started down the stairs two or three at a time. I was nearly to the bottom when I stopped. My father and Stricter were waiting for me. I had left them standing on the sidewalk while I went off to prove my manhood, or something like that, and I was about to walk out of the yellow light with nothing to show for it. I reached in my pocket. I had thirteen dollars: two crumpled-up fives and three ones. I put eight dollars back in my pocket and hit the opening to the stairwell on the run, waving the other five like a flag of triumph. I ran across the street and put the money in Stricter's hand.

He looked at it and said, "How'd you do it?"

"I just asked her for it."

I thought I said it with a great air of confidence. I was cool.

My father said, "You took a long time just to ask. You sure you didn't ask for anything else while you were up there?"

I got indignant. "No, sir!"

My father and Stricter smiled at each other.

Stricter said, "I'm impressed. You could have a career as a bill collector."

He shook hands with my father and said, "Enjoyed our talk." He walked away toward the lot where he always parked his car.

My father said, "I've got to get on the road, or your mother's going to spend most of the night worrying about me. I'll give you a lift."

"That's okay. You're going the other way. It's not far."

We shook hands, and he got in his car. Just before he pulled out of the parking place, when he had his head out of the window and was looking back for traffic, he looked across the street and upstairs at the curtained windows over the hardware store. A figure passed in front of one of them, then the window shade was pulled the rest of the way down. My father looked at me and again at the windows upstairs across the street and drove away laughing, his voice, high and loud on the chill wind, funneled up the street.

I watched his taillights disappear around the corner and stepped back onto the sidewalk. I turned up the collar on my jacket, hunched into the wind, and walked to my rooming house. Every time a car passed me, I watched its taillights glow in the darkness. It seemed I still could hear his laughter echoing up the wide street. He had more than a hundred miles to go before he got home, and I thought he'd probably laugh all the way. For the life of me, I couldn't figure out what my father thought was so damned funny.

THE CHILL

THE WOMEN WANTED to go for a Sunday drive. Elizabeth, my mother-in-law, wanted to go all the way to Petit Jean Mountain. I thought a little drive up to Morrilton, which was on the way to the mountain, would be good enough. We went north out of Conway through the valley toward Morrilton. Most of the year, it's a beautiful drive, but in early March, signs of winter still override the first movements of spring, and it's not very pretty in the valley. There was some greening, but the hardwoods were still bare of leaves, stark and gray in the slanting light. The road was narrow—two lanes of blacktop—but good, not rough even though it had a few stomach-churning spots, like the curves on Beckett's Hill and the old wooden bridge across Coffman's Creek, especially in bad weather. Goldie and I sat in the front, and Elizabeth took the back seat for herself. She liked that because she could sit in the middle and look out both sides, never mind how many times I asked her not to block my vision in the rearview mirror.

Goldie said, "Look, Momma, there's a hawk up on the top of that post."

Elizabeth said, "Where?"

Goldie said, "We just passed it, but I saw it."

Elizabeth said, "It was probably hunting for something."

I just kept on driving. I didn't have time to look at birds and scenery. I had come up behind an eighteen-wheeler ahead, and I wanted to get around it before I got stuck behind it going up Beckett's Hill. I let an oncoming car go past, then I pulled out, pushed the gas pedal to the floor, and kicked the old Dodge into passing gear. I got around that big rig with room to spare.

Elizabeth said, "You don't have to drive so fast."

I looked in the rearview mirror and saw her leaning against the back of the seat. She had her arms spread wide, with a hand pressed against each side of the car, like she needed something to hold her in.

"Had to hurry to get around that one. Didn't want to be behind him on the hill."

Elizabeth said, "I can't see anything when you go so fast."

I looked to the road. I had to pass the truck, and we were coming up to the old wooden bridge over Coffman's Creek. I slowed down for that one. I didn't know just how old the bridge was, but it was old. Too old. Driving across that bridge made the car sound and feel like it was running over a stretched-out washboard.

Goldie said, "Look, Ernest, how high the water in the creek is. It's already almost to the bottom of the bridge."

She was right. The water was high, and I wished we had stayed home, but wishing doesn't change anything. I eased my worry some by noting that we were almost to Morrilton, and I felt sure we had time to stop and get a cup of coffee and a piece of pie.

I said, "I thought we'd stop in Morrilton for some pie."

Elizabeth said, "Aren't we going to the mountain?"

Goldie said, "It's too far."

"Too far for what?"

"We couldn't get back till after dark."

Elizabeth said, "There's nothing to see in Morrilton."

She was almost right. Morrilton wasn't much more than a couple of grease spots along the road. There was one traffic light, but if you caught it green and blinked twice, you didn't see much of Morrilton.

"Damnation!"

A black panel truck passed me in the middle of the last curve going into Morrilton and barely made it back across the yellow line before an oncoming pickup flashed by.

I said, "There's some crazy people on the road."

Goldie said, "That was close."

Elizabeth said, "Drive careful, Ernest."

"I am. I am."

The café was right across from the old train depot and served homemade pies good as I ever found. It had good coffee too. I knew I didn't have to talk Goldie into a snack, and I figured that if we dallied long enough, Elizabeth would realize it was too late to go the rest of the way to the mountain. I pulled into the small parking lot and stopped. When we got out of the car, the air was cooler than it was when we left the house, and the sky was darker. The gray overcast was heavier. Beyond the depot, a tall line of clouds was changing from purple to black.

We sat in a booth up against the big plate glass window in the front so we could see what was going on outside. There wasn't much traffic to watch even though the road was the US highway going to Fort Smith and Oklahoma. I knew that road well. I had driven it often enough, straight over, turning off up to Tulsa, up farther into Kansas, to Wichita. That was where I first met Goldie and Elizabeth too, more than twenty years before. I looked out the window and knew I had decided right about not going farther than Morrilton that day.

The waitress came to our booth, and Goldie ordered ice cream with her pie. She blushed a little bit because I smiled at her when she did it. It sounded so good I ordered the same thing.

I said, "We'll get fat together."

Goldie said, "I'm not getting fat."

"OK," I said. "Pleasingly plump."

Elizabeth said, "Why do you want to make her fat?"

"It's not my idea," I said.

Goldie said, "Momma, we're just joking."

Elizabeth told the waitress, "I'd like a cup of hot tea with an order of light toast."

She wasn't smiling. She sat against the window and watched the first huge drops of rain splatter against the glass and run down. It was a hard rain that came on fast. The sky turned like it was late evening, and the rain drummed against the window. Elizabeth watched it. She seemed almost in a spell. I felt good. I was glad I wasn't driving in the weather, and I was inside in a neat, warm, lighted café with Goldie and my piece of pie à la mode. Dutch apple.

Elizabeth said, "I used to like to watch the rain. When I lived at Aunt Fern's, it was upstairs over Uncle Tony's store, and she had a big window. The rain hit against it, and the wind rattled it sometimes so hard I thought it would break. The sky got so black it was like night, and everybody was terribly afraid of tornadoes. We used to sit on the back porch in Wichita and watch three or four at a time moving high up in the sky, off toward the west. I was almost in one once, but that was before Goldie was born. We didn't used to have so many tornadoes when I was really young. Seems like we have them all the time now."

Goldie said, "Momma, what are you talking about?"

"When I was young, even before I met Bill, even before I met Frank—he was my first husband—"

She was wandering. She did that more and more lately. Goldie looked down at her pie and ice cream. Her bottom lip trembled. She put her fork down beside her plate.

I said, "Aren't you going to finish your pie?"

"I'm not hungry."

Elizabeth said, "It's a sin to waste food."

I said, "Who ever told you that?"

"It is. It's a sin to waste food when children in China are starving."

She used to say that all the time when my children were little, but I hadn't heard her say it for a long time. Goldie took a deep breath and pulled herself up against the back of the booth. Elizabeth looked at the rain striking the window. I watched her, and I thought there was something different about her, a look I hadn't seen but maybe a hint of before. She stared at the rain, but I thought for sure she was looking at something beyond the rain.

Elizabeth used to be a striking figure of a woman. She was tall, nearly five eleven, and she had sharp, angular features with a full head of salt-and-pepper hair. She used to be hefty, not fat, just big. I often wondered how Bill, Goldie's father and Elizabeth's second husband, managed to handle her because she was almost a head taller and thirty pounds heavier than he was, rest his soul. But she had grown thin the last five or six years, and sometimes just looking at the thin folds of flesh gathered on her neck and her arms made me feel a kind of sadness. And she wandered in her mind. I didn't think she had ever talked to anyone who wasn't there yet, but sometimes she lost the drift of a conversation and blurted out comments or questions that had nothing to do with the subject at hand. Or at other times, usually in the evening after supper, if we were watching television, she just started talking about things from the past, and if she started jumping from one subject to the other, Goldie had to get up and leave the room because it hurt her so to see Elizabeth with the wanderings.

Once, I said, "She's just getting old."

Goldie had said, "Sometimes when she wanders, I'm afraid she won't come back. It's almost like she doesn't want to come back, sometimes."

That's why Goldie didn't finish her pie à la mode in Morrilton that day. She trembled—you could hardly see it—like she had been caught by a chill. The trembling left as fast as it came, but I knew the chill was still there and would be there until tonight, with me up against her back and two extra blankets piled on before she would get to sleep.

The rain slackened to a light drizzle, and we hurried to the car. As I waited to pull onto the highway, a large deep rumble of thunder filled the air; the rain became a deluge again. Sheets and sheets of water poured down. The wipers hardly did any good at all. I thought about pulling back into the parking lot and waiting it out, but I thought, too, about Coffman's Creek that was already full and that old wooden bridge I knew I wouldn't even try to cross if there was water running over it. At least, I didn't have to explain about not going to the mountain.

Goldie said, "Is it safe to drive?"

"Sure," I said. "It's just a little rain."

Elizabeth said, "For God's sake, be careful, Bill."

I was halfway onto the road when it registered that she had called me Bill, and I pulled across the oncoming lane, turned left, and drove toward home. Like I said, Bill was Goldie's father and Elizabeth's second husband. He died of throat cancer fourteen years before. I got along with him all right, but I always had thought he liked his beer too much. So far as I knew, he never saved a nickel. We were a half mile down the road before Goldie said anything.

"Momma, you called Ernest, Bill."

Elizabeth didn't answer. I watched her now and then in the rearview mirror. She sat up straight, leaned a little forward, and aimed her eyes dead ahead. Goldie squirmed a little, wanting and waiting for her momma to answer her. She acted like she was afraid to look back to see Elizabeth. I looked in my mirror at Elizabeth looking straight back at me. Something strange in her eyes made me think she was seeing things, people maybe, that no one else could see. It gave me a shiver.

Elizabeth must have been watching me because she asked, "Are you all right? You're not catching a cold, are you?"

I turned to answer her, "No, no. I'm fine."

She said, "Ernest, what's that man doing in the middle of the road?"

A state trooper all decked out in a yellow slicker stopped us at the bridge at Coffman's Creek. He said, "It is safe, one car at a time, stay in the middle, and go slow." I did all that, came off the other side, and figured I had it made with just the big grade down Beckett's Hill, and eleven miles of ordinary road into Conway and home. The rain was falling lighter, and I felt good. I shouldn't have forgotten my motto: YANGIM (you ain't never got it made). In fact, in just a little less than a mile everything, I mean, damned near *everything*, started coming undone.

The small upgrade on that side of Beckett's Hill was clear. Only one oncoming car passed us, and none was going our way in front of us. The grade was really a gentle slope that led to a rounded crest that looked like it would slope off on the other side the same way. You had to get right up on the top to see how steep and crooked the way down was. Twenty yards down the steep side, a big sign warned truck drivers of the grade and to use low gear.

Almost halfway down the hill, I heard an air horn. In the mirror, past Elizabeth's head—she still stared straight to the front—I saw the tractor trailer coming too fast. He was already in the other lane to pass me and leaning on his horn. I looked ahead and saw we weren't far from the next curve, a sharp left turn that barely straightened out before it went back right just as sharp. Goldie turned around in the seat. I don't know if she said anything. I heard only the air horn. I had my foot on the brake, and both hands were hard on the steering wheel. The car started to skid. I don't know if I was breathing. The tractor trailer pulled beside me, went past us, pulled back into the right lane, started into the curve, and jackknifed.

Now that was a sight! I'm surprised my hair didn't turn white watching that big rig sway back and forth across the road, then suddenly swing around in a big arc. The trailer came around to meet the tractor, which looked like it was swinging from the other way. Both of them—the tractor and the trailer—slid sideways down the road, into the curve, and, lucky for the driver, into the side of the hill instead of off and down the drop on the left side of the road. My car hit something, some kind of extra-slick spot, and the skid became a slide going out of control. It wasn't much, but it was enough to turn us so that we ended up across the road and only a matter of inches from the wheels of the trailer.

We sat there for a minute, crossways in the road, while I caught my breath. Goldie, more or less, picked herself up off the floor and the seat. Her glasses had come off, and she fussed with them to get them back on. Elizabeth sat straight up, leaning a little forward, looking straight ahead. She looked as if she hadn't moved, but something had happened. It showed in the tautness of her face and, again, especially in her eyes. They had color and depth, but a strange kind of depth, as though her eyes caught and held on to images no one else could see. Goldie got her glasses on and turned to see about Elizabeth, and I thought about the driver in the tractor. His side of the cab had slammed pretty hard against the hill.

I had on a light windbreaker that once upon a time had been waterproof. The rain acted like it saw me coming when I stepped out of the car and came down heavy again. It didn't take long for me to be soaked. It was a cold rain, and I felt myself shivering as I moved about. The cab was so high I couldn't see into it from the ground. I climbed up on the passenger side and looked in. The driver was a young fellow. I thought he hadn't had enough experience to be pulling a rig like that in bad weather. He beat on his steering wheel with both fists and cursed. I opened the door, and he turned and looked at me like I must have surprised him from outer space. His two clenched fists were frozen in the air above the wheel.

I said, "Are you all right?"

"I'm fine," he said.

"Can I help you? Are you hurt?"

"I'm all right!" he said and grabbed his side when he tried to move. I gave him a hand to pull on, and he worked his way across the seat toward me. He obviously had more than a little bit of pain, and I expected he had some cracked ribs. I heard a siren and looked back up the road.

The young fellow said, "I already called the state police on my radio."

The trooper who had been at Coffman's Creek was there about as quick as he could have been, but that didn't keep us from having a long delay before we got on our way again. It took three hours to get a wrecker out there and move the trailer enough to open up one lane of traffic. I spent most of that time standing in the cold rain, watching the proceedings, or sitting in the trooper's car giving my official statement. By the time I got back in my own car again, I was wet, cold, tired, and halfway to being sick. The night had gone about as dark as I ever thought dark could get. The rain beating on the top of the car and the *clack, clack* of the wipers pressed on a raw nerve in the back of my head. I was going to be in bad shape for hitting the road the next morning. Goldie had climbed into the back seat with Elizabeth, who was leaning back against the seat with her eyes closed and her mouth open. I couldn't tell if she was breathing.

I asked, "Is she all right?"

Goldie said, "No, she's not."

"Is she hurt?"

"She's not injured. She's hurting, though."

"That slip and slide we did must've scared the hell out of her."

Goldie said, "It did me."

Goldie had taken off her coat and wrapped it around Elizabeth like it was a blanket. She wiped at a drop of spittle that oozed out of her mother's mouth and tucked the coat around her to make her warm.

The rain stopped a half mile before we got into town. I was amazed by the debris on and along the road—limbs and trash blown by the storm. I wondered if maybe a little twister hadn't come through the area. As we drove into town, I had to navigate around tree debris and some pieces of roofing blown off nearby houses. A lot of water had collected in the low spots, and some streets were flooded. A sound like a moan came from the back seat. I looked back. Elizabeth was trying to move around. Goldie held the coat on her to keep her still. We were within a couple of blocks of the house.

I said, "We're almost there."

When I pulled into the driveway at the back of the house, I didn't go all the way into the garage. That made it easier to open the door and get Elizabeth out of the car. I turned off the motor, and Elizabeth jerked upright.

She said, "Are we there?"

Goldie said, "We're home, Momma."

Elizabeth said, "We're in Topeka already?"

I said, "No, Elizabeth. Topeka's in Kansas. We're in Arkansas."

"What are we doing in Arkansas?"

"We live here, Momma."

"I don't live in Arkansas."

"Yes you do, Momma. We all do."

"I'm not going to Arkansas."

"Momma, you're already here. Let's go inside, and I'll make some tea."

Elizabeth said, "I'd like some tea. Want some tea, Bill?"

I acted like I didn't notice her calling me Bill and said, "Hot tea sounds good, Elizabeth."

What I really wanted was to get inside and get on some dry clothes. The wet and cold in my clothes felt like it had soaked all the way to the bone. I helped Goldie pull Elizabeth out of the car, and together—one on each side—we walked her up the back steps and into the house.

Goldie said, "Let's go to the front."

Elizabeth slept in the front bedroom that had a tall window and that opened onto the front porch. She liked to sit in the window when the weather was too cool for her to go onto the porch. We guided her to sit on the bed.

Goldie turned to me and said, "You go change."

Elizabeth said, "Where's Aunt Fern?"

I stood and looked at her, but Goldie said, "You go change. You'll catch your death if you don't get out of those wet clothes."

Elizabeth said, "Tell Tony to come here."

Goldie said, "Go on!"

She meant me. I went to the back to our room, undressed, took a steaming shower, and put on dry clothes. I went into the kitchen and saw that Goldie had already heated water for tea, and I made myself a cup and took it with me into Elizabeth's bedroom.

Elizabeth lay in the bed, her eyes closed, her long, angular body outlined under the blanket Goldie had spread over her. Goldie motioned me to leave the room, and she came with me into the kitchen.

"She should sleep straight through the night," Goldie said.

I asked, "Does she know where she is?"

"I don't think so."

"Does she really think she's in Topeka?"

Goldie nodded. Her lower lip quivered and sent a tremor through her body.

She pulled herself away from the trembling and said, "You must be hungry."

"What about you?"

"Me too. Go get your things together for tomorrow, and I'll fix something."

I went into our bedroom, pulled my suitcase out from under the bed, and laid it open. I packed and counted everything I would need for a week, five days really. I fixed a suit in a hanging bag and set out one to wear the next morning. From time to time, I heard Goldie moving around in the kitchen, but she hadn't called me by the time I finished packing everything except the shaving stuff I would put in in the morning. I closed the suitcase, set it against a wall, and went through the short hall to Elizabeth's room.

Her eyes were open. Goldie had left a small lamp turned on beside the bed. It was a soft light, made even softer by a heavy fabric shade. Elizabeth lay still. I watched her breathe and wondered what she was thinking. It was hard to believe she was lying there convinced she was in Topeka or waiting for Uncle Tony, who had died before I had ever met Elizabeth. It was hard to see her eyes in the soft light. She stared at the ceiling, but I knew she was not looking at the ceiling. I asked myself what she saw and where her mind had taken her. Where was it likely to go next? What would I do if she really became an invalid? I wasn't ready for that. And I thought she might die. *She might die*! In *my* house! Right here, and I couldn't be ready for that. There were sounds behind me, and Goldie touched my arm.

She whispered, "Your supper's ready."

"She's awake," I said.

"Maybe."

I said, "Her eyes are open."

She said, "She's all right."

"Should you call the doctor?"

"Maybe in the morning, if she isn't better. I don't think she's hurt. She's just confused. Let's get something to eat."

I followed her to the kitchen. We ate supper without ceremony or conversation. When we finished, I washed the dishes and put them to drain so Goldie could go to see about Elizabeth. I remembered the pot of coffee I had made and poured a cup. I sipped half of it and threw the rest away. I started outside just to walk and remembered how wet it was out there. I went to the front and found Goldie sitting in Elizabeth's rocking chair. I pulled a straight-back chair up beside her. I don't know how long we sat there. We didn't talk, or if we did, it wasn't about anything that mattered. We stayed there until Elizabeth started to snore. I looked at her. Her eyes were closed again. In a moment, she turned onto her side and pulled her knees up almost to her chest. She started making little sounds, like muttering, not really talking, and I figured she was dreaming.

I said, "Let's go to bed."

Goldie got up and tucked the blanket around Elizabeth, brushed her mother's hair back, and wiped her brow with a tissue.

Then she said, "All right. I think we can go to bed now."

Later, I lay awake thinking about Elizabeth and wondering if even in her dreams, she was traveling old, worn roads that had become such deep ruts in her memory she might not be able to get out of them. Goldie was awake too. I could tell by her breathing. I reached over and touched her on the shoulder, and she scooted toward me. I moved myself up close to her back and held her in one arm.

I said, "Everything's going to be all right."

Goldie said, "I'm cold. I'm so cold."

I pulled up an extra blanket to cover us both. I heard Elizabeth cough. I raised up and waited a moment to listen for more sounds that would signal a need for one of us to go check on her. It stayed quiet.

Goldie didn't move when she asked, "Do I need to go see about her?"

I said, "No. She's quiet now. Go to sleep. It's all right. You'll see. Everything's going to be all right."

I lay again against Goldie's back with one arm around her and prayed she would forgive me for the lie I had just told.

A WIDE DAY

WILL STUFFED HIS hands in his pockets and leaned against the wall of the bus station in Conway. He looked angry. I figured he was pissed because our father had sent him to meet my bus, and it was after midnight. As soon as he saw me, he turned without any sort of greeting and walked to where he had parked our father's car. He opened the trunk, and I threw the single gym bag I had packed into it.

Will said, "Is that all you got?"

"It's enough. I don't plan to stay long."

He slammed down the trunk lid.

"You're lucky."

When we got in the car, Will added, "You're gonna wish you hadn't come home." Then he burned rubber and sent a loud squeal hurtling through the silence of the dark town. He turned onto College Street in front of the Catholic church, hit the accelerator, and went nearly airborne over the hump that held the railroad tracks.

I said, "What's your problem?"

"Nothing."

He pushed hard on the accelerator and drove through the stop sign at the next corner.

I said, "What the hell?"

Will didn't look at me. He didn't turn his head, but I could tell he wasn't exactly paying attention to the road either. We had almost a mile to go without any more stop signs or any turns to make. I'd driven the same street the same way many times. There almost never was anyone else out and about that late at night. We made that nearly a mile in no time, and Will slammed on the brakes.

As he turned the corner onto the street where he and our parents lived, Will said, "He wants to move again."

He meant our father. What he said didn't surprise me. Will and I both had decided when we were even a lot younger that moving probably was what our father did best.

"When?"

"Just as soon as they get Grandma in the ground."

"Why do you think so?"

We were only three or four blocks from the house, and he turned the corner onto Watkins Street too fast, again sending a high squeal through the clear night air.

He said, "Shit. I don't *think* so. I know it. He's going to move, and I'm going to have to go with him. I'll bet you're not home ten minutes before you know it too. You better be careful, 'cause he's going to try to talk you into going too. I heard him talking to Mother about it."

When we drove into our driveway, our father stood in the backyard, waiting in a square of yellowish light that spread outward from the kitchen window. He glared at Will as we walked toward the house. He clenched and unclenched his fists—his sure sign of anger about to get the best of him. When our father started to say something, Will stopped and turned toward me.

"Go ahead. I'll get your bag."

I shook hands with my father. We didn't hug. He wasn't a hugger. He told me how glad he was I had come and how anxious my mother was to see me, and all the time, he glared at Will walking back to the car in the driveway.

I asked, "How's Grandma?"

"She's hanging on. The doctor can't figure out why she's still here. Don't feel shocked if she doesn't know who you are."

As we climbed the steps to the back door, Will came up behind us.

Our father said, "From the sounds I heard when you turned the corner, you must've been in some kind of hurry. Money for tires doesn't grow on trees."

Will said, "You talked all evening about how you wished Mark would hurry up and get here. So I hurried."

He walked through the back door I had opened and told me, "I'll put your bag in the bedroom. You get the cot."

Our father put a hand on my shoulder and urged me into the house, and he said, "I swear to Christ I don't know what to do with him. He acts like he's mad at the world all the time."

Mother came through the door leading into the back bedroom, put her arms out to hug me, and said, "My big boy. I'm glad you're here. Your grandma will be glad too."

When the hug was finished, I said, "Dad said she might not recognize me."

She turned her head—or did she? Maybe just her eyes moved. My father stood still. I could not have told you even right then exactly how it happened. I only knew her light-blue eyes had, in an instant, stopped my father where he stood with the back door still half-open, letting June bugs and moths attracted by the light fly into the kitchen.

Growing up with them, I had long since learned to fear my father's voice, his blood-darkened face, and the threat of his wide, thick hand, even though it had hardly ever struck me. Though his hand and his voice threatened, nothing he ever said or did could stop either him or me to change the atmosphere of a room or define the mood of a whole day the way my mother could with her *look*.

A glance emphasized by one raised eyebrow used to make me try to crawl inside myself and hide away like a thief looking for the darkest part of night. My father simply stood still and looked down at his feet as Mother turned me toward the door that led to the other side of the house.

"Come see your grandmother. She'll be happy you came," she said to me. Then to my father, she added, "Shut the door, Ernest. You're letting all the bugs in."

My father was right. My grandmother did not recognize me. Her eyes fluttered open now and then, and she mumbled something unintelligible. My mother held her ear close to my grandmother's mouth and waited longer than I could comfortably hold my breath before she stood up and wiped moisture from the side of her face with her sleeve.

"She was trying to say something."

"I couldn't hear anything."

"Maybe if you spoke to her, just to let her know you're here."

I did. I spoke loud and slow, the way I would speak to a small child in order to be understood or how I imagined I should speak to an old person hard of hearing. I said my name, told her she looked beautiful, and that I had come home just to see her. I told her I couldn't wait to have a cup of tea with her. She opened her eyes and stared at the ceiling, then came the sound of something like air being let slowly out of the squeezed opening of a balloon, and I jerked backward from the ammoniac sting of the smell of urine.

My mother turned toward a small chest against the wall. She pulled out a fresh nightgown from one drawer and clean sheets from another. She held the sheets to her face and took a deep breath.

Mother said, "She always liked the way sheets smelled after they'd been hung out in the sun." She laid them down at the foot of the bed and added, "Go tell your father I need him."

My father stepped into the room and said, "I'm right here."

They started to change my grandmother's clothes and sheets, and I decided I needed, right then, to put my bag in my room.

The house was small and divided down the middle. On one side were the kitchen and the living room large enough to include a dining room table. On the other side, a bedroom in the back and another in the front were connected by a hall, off of which were the bathroom and another very small bedroom. The small bedroom was Will's and mine. Will was in the bed. Somebody had put up a folding canvas cot under the single window in the room for me. It left little space for walking, but a full moon lighted the room through the window. I squeezed my way to the cot, got undressed, and stretched out.

Will said, "Did you ever see anything like it? She's like a breathing skeleton."

Being home and getting in bed had not softened the anger out of Will's voice.

I said, "I don't think she knew I was there."

"She doesn't know anything, man. You're lucky you're not still living here."

I looked through the window at the moon and tried to remember all the things my grandmother had told me about it when I was little—the man in the moon, green cheese, werewolves, and other madnesses inspired by a full moon. She loved to tell scary stories.

Will said, "You ought to come back and stay for a while."

"I have a job. Someday, I'm out of here." He pulled the covers up and turned away from me. I was nearly settled into the depression in the center of the cot when he raised his head and added, "And soon too."

I had had a long day at work and a four-hour ride on a bus. It was well after midnight. I fell asleep, too tired to even dream.

I looked into the bright light of a sun well up when loud voices coming down the hall from another part of the house woke me.

"Goddamn it, Goldie. You're being unreasonable."

"I don't care."

"You don't know what you're asking."

"My daddy died with nobody there, and I'm not going to let that happen to Momma."

"That was a county hospital. It was because he was a charity case. We'd be paying this time."

"How? We can't pay all of the grocery bill this month. I told you not to start buying groceries on credit."

"We'd pay it, maybe a little bit at a time. It would be different."

"You can't be sure of that."

"I'd make sure."

"No, Ernest. No!"

Her footsteps on the wooden floor in the hall sounded like rocks hitting the wall. His footfalls, slower and weighted, followed hers. Then the front screen door slammed, and I knew he had gone outside onto the porch. In a minute, the porch swing creaked rhythmically, punctuated by the sound of his shoes tapping the floor.

Will was not in his bed. I grabbed my pants, put them on, and hurried to the bathroom. I relieved myself, dashed cold water on my face, and combed my hair. I looked in the mirror and decided I didn't need to shave. A light beard was something I inherited from my father, and I still could go a day or two without a razor. To avoid going through my grandmother's room, I went through the back bedroom into the kitchen and then to the front and out onto the porch.

My father said, "I was wondering how late you were going to sleep."

I looked at my watch. It said nearly half past nine.

"I was tired."

"I didn't know selling shoes was that hard on you."

I said, "It's not. It was the bus ride." And I walked down the steps into the small front yard and looked at the dogwood tree in full bloom across the street.

He said, "I'm thinking about planting tomatoes along the fence in the back this year."

"That will be nice."

"It's early yet. In another month, it should be right. We'll have them for summer."

I remembered Will's anger from last night, and I said, "Are you going to still be here then?"

He stopped the motion of the swing.

"What makes you ask that?"

"Will thinks you're getting ready to move again."

He kicked the floor hard, and the chains holding up the swing trembled.

"Maybe."

"So who'll pick the tomatoes if you're not here?"

The chains on the swing creaked louder, and his foot stomped once on the floor.

"The landlord can have the goddamned things for all I care."

I don't know where his small outburst might have gone, but it stopped cold when Mother walked out onto the porch.

She said, "I called Dr. Roblyer. He said he'd come by and see her this afternoon."

My father said, "Good. I want to talk to him."

They glared at each other for a long moment until my mother turned to me and said, "Good morning, sleepyhead." Then she looked again at my father and said, "Ernest, if you want chicken for dinner this afternoon, you need to kill one—maybe two." And again she turned to me and said, "Mark, why don't you say good morning to your grandmother?"

That was not really a request. I followed my mother into the house and into my grandmother's bedroom. It occurred to me right then that I wished I had been awake earlier so I could have gone with Will, wherever he went.

My mother said, "You can keep her company. I just changed her a few minutes ago. Why don't you talk to her? She always loved to talk with you."

Why don't I talk to her? Simple answer was I was afraid to be alone in the room with my grandmother. What if something happened? What if she died? At eighteen, I didn't know what dying would look like. I had only seen one other corpse in my life, and that was my father's father. But he had been dead for a couple of days already and was all dressed up and made-up, lying on a white satin pillow. Three years before this. I was Will's age then. Would it be different from that? What did a dead body look like lying in an ordinary bed meant for someone still alive? I poked my head into her room. Her eyes were closed. I watched her breathe, and I thought, *Maybe I can just go join Father in the backyard where he is killing a chicken.*

My father could wring a chicken's neck with a couple of flicks of his wrist. When I was little, I liked to sit on the backdoor steps and watch the chicken run around the yard, its head flopping from one side to the other. I don't know what it was, but it scared me and made me laugh at the same time.

My father said, "If you ever wondered how dumb a chicken is, the damned thing doesn't even know it's dead."

One time, a chicken jumped, flapped, flopped, and fell right in front of my feet. It trembled and then was still. I tried to measure the time between the trembling and the stillness, and I couldn't. It trembled. It lay still. It was alive. It was dead. That's when I realized there is no time, no anything, between being alive and being dead. Would it be that way with my grandmother? Grandma opened her eyes, and I stayed in the room.

Grandma's eyes followed me as I walked around the foot of the bed and came up beside her. Did she smile? Her lips moved, and I bent over as my mother had and put my ear close to her face. I heard whisperings—or was it just the struggle of air to move in and out?—and leaned closer, until my ear almost touched her lips. The sounds were like thin water running over pebbles or like small dry leaves stirred by a breeze. I stood and wiped my ear with my handkerchief.

I told her, "The dogwoods are blooming. The tree across the street is almost finished."

She closed her eyes. I watched her breathe. There was neither motion nor sound between her breaths. There was only time. I felt dizzy and realized I had been holding my breath every time she took in one until she finally let it out. I couldn't think of anything else to say or do, and I'm certain my mother saw a wide look of relief on my face when she came into the room and told me she had put some breakfast on the table for me.

"After you eat, you can help Daddy in the kitchen. He's already killed the chickens. I can watch her."

Her mood had changed. I knew that when she said "Daddy" instead of "your father." My father didn't refuse my help. He talked to me while I quartered potatoes and peeled onions and did whatever else he pointed out for me to do. He was good in the kitchen, better than my mother was. He liked to spend late Sunday mornings preparing a huge dinner for midafternoon. It kept him from going to church with Mother.

As I chopped some onions, he started to tell what he and my mother had been arguing about earlier. He wanted to have my grandmother put in the hospital. She could be more comfortable there. People who knew how to take care of someone dying would be there. Mother had decided she would keep my grandmother at home. He had not found a way to turn her mind to another direction. Mother didn't realize how unreasonable she was being and how hard it was to do *this thing* she was asking him to do. He didn't know what he would do if Grandma died while he was watching her—and how would he know she was really dead anyway?

He said Dr. Roblyer told him to just take a small hand mirror and hold it up close to—but not touching—Grandma's mouth and her nose and then hold it there for a minute or so. My father said he wanted to know just how damned long *or so* would be. Anyway, hold it there and wait, and if the glass was clear when he pulled it away, if there was no moisture on the mirror, then my grandmother would be dead. There wouldn't be any need to call the doctor. Just make a note of what time it was—approximately would be good enough—and call the funeral home, and someone would come and take my grandmother away. The doctor could sign the death certificate later.

My father held a wooden spoon while he talked about holding the mirror close to my grandmother's face to look for the moisture of breath. His hand shook so hard he sprayed the stovetop with gravy drippings.

Dinner was tense. Will did not come home. Mother said he spent Sundays at his girlfriend's house. She and my father both acted as though it wasn't possible to do enough for the other one.

"Would you like some gravy?"

"No, thank you."

"Did it get cold?"

"It's fine. I just don't—"

"I can heat it up for you."

"No, that's all right. You've done enough. I appreciate it. Maybe Mark wants his heated."

I said, "No, it's okay, really."

I have recalled that hour many times. It took me a long time to get the understanding I have now about what was happening between them. Tension between them wasn't anything new. Growing up, I had sat through interminable silent dinners just waiting for some kind of eruption. But this time was different. This time, it wasn't just stubbornness or hurt feelings because he or she couldn't have his or her way, or because one had flung a real or imagined barb at the other. This time, it was fear. They were afraid—I was afraid—that my grandmother would die alone while we ate dinner. I knew that then. What I didn't know then was we all feared she wouldn't die soon, that she would take too long to reach those two points between which there is no time. Our fear made the gravy get cold. It plugged the holes in the saltshaker. Still, we pretended.

My mother asked, "How's your work? Are you selling lots of shoes?"

I said, "I'm selling some. I don't think it's what I want to do for the rest of my life."

She said, "It's a good job. Don't be too quick to give it up."

"No, ma'am."

My grandmother had a name for a day filled with tension that had everybody wondering when it would be over. She called it a wide day. This one promised to be a very wide day.

Dr. Roblyer came very late in the afternoon. He went with my mother into the front bedroom, and my father and I waited on the front porch. He sat in the swing, and I sat on the top step. We were out there maybe ten minutes when I spotted Will walking up the street. He was limping. I looked back to the swing and saw my father was watching him too.

He said, "What did Will do now?"

Will stopped by Dr. Roblyer's Cadillac parked on the street in front of the house. He put his face against the window to look inside, and when he turned to come up the path to the porch, he limped and carried one shoe in his hand.

My father said, "What the hell happened to you?"

His voice came out hard, like Will getting hurt was another straw on the camel's already overloaded back.

Will said, "We went climbing the bluffs out at the river. We wanted to see the eagle's nests. I fell. Ain't nothing broken though."

He hobbled up and sat down beside me before he said, "Is she dead yet?"

My father lunged out of the swing and shouted, "What kind of goddamned question is that?"

He took only a couple of steps toward us, but that was enough to have Will already up and backing away from him. I thought he was going to turn and run, but he stumbled and his face twisted with pain. He sat on the path and looked up at our father.

Will said, "I saw the doctor's car, and I thought something had happened."

I moved down the steps, reached out a hand, and said, "Here."

Will allowed me to pull him to his feet and help him hobble to the porch.

My father said, "Sit there. I'll get the doctor to look at your ankle."

When our father disappeared into the house, Will said, "Jesus, I didn't mean anything."

I said, "He's scared. He's never been around anyone dying before."

"Shit. Who has?"

Dr. Robyler came outside with our mother and father and knelt down to look at Will's ankle. He laid Will's foot in one hand and gently probed the swollen flesh with his fingers. Will's leg jerked. The doctor told Will to come to his office in the morning for x-rays. And in the meantime, he should stay off it, keep it elevated, and maybe put some ice on it.

My mother said, "I have an ice bag." And she went back into the house.

Will stood, leaned on me, and hobbled up the steps and across the porch to the screen door. As we went, I heard the doctor tell my father, "I don't know what's keeping her going, Mr. Rambler, but it can't be long now. It just can't be."

"I don't know how I'm going to do this."

"You'll do fine, Mr. Rambler. Just do exactly as I told you. You'll be just fine."

He started to go, turned back, and added, "Your wife seems awfully tired. Make her sleep tonight. If I haven't heard anything, I'll call in the morning."

Through the screen door, I saw my father standing alone in the path as the doctor went to his car and drove away. My father looked smaller, his shoulders slumped; and when he turned to come back to the porch, he moved slowly, like someone measuring the effort it took to lift a leg and put one foot in front of the other. At that moment, whatever else in the world he might believe, he did not believe he would be *just fine*.

Will hobbled to his bed. Mother worried over him and put an ice pack on his ankle. Afterward, she gave me the choice of watching my grandmother or making the sandwiches for our supper. I made the sandwiches. She went into the front bedroom, and my father sat in the porch swing and waited.

Will's course for the evening and night was clearly set, but the rest of us were trying to find our separate ways to make it until next morning.

I went several times into my grandmother's room. Her breathing seemed even slower, but it was also louder, like someone gargling, only from deeper than the throat. We could hear it even on the porch.

My father said, "It's the rattle."

"The what?"

"The death rattle. I've never heard it before, but I remember people talking about it when one of my uncles died. They said it lasted for days."

He quickly changed the subject and asked questions about my work and my life in Hot Springs. I assured him my life was rather dull, and my work was neither more nor less than what I expected it to be. Selling shoes at Stricter's Discount Fashion Shoe Store was my first job combined with living away from home. I lived in a furnished room, ate all my meals in greasy spoon restaurants, and without a car, I had little or no social life. Yes, I had met a girl; but no, it wasn't serious. We usually walked to a movie on Sunday afternoons. I assumed he knew I wasn't telling him everything and that he didn't really want me to tell him everything.

He said, "Stick with it. Something will work out." I didn't know whether he was talking about the job or the girl or his intention to move.

After we had sat quietly for what felt like a long while, he said, "I don't know what to do with Will."

I looked at the stars. The sky was clear, and the crescent moon shone bright.

He said, "I'm gone all week. Your mother has to deal with him, and he's in a new kind of trouble every time I call home. He almost got suspended from school last week for fighting."

"Will's afraid you're going to move again."

My father pushed the swing harder. Sheet lightning brightened the sky in the distance.

He said, "The Arkansas territory isn't as good as it used to be. People aren't buying like they were when I first came here."

That was only a little over a year before.

I said, "Will wants to stay here and graduate."

He said, "I don't know." And after three or four squeaks of the swing, he said, "I'm thinking about going to Chicago. There's more opportunity there. You could sell a lot more shoes up there."

I don't think he took a breath between those last two sentences.

I said, "I don't think I want to go to some other new place so soon."

My mother called to him right then, and he got up off the swing.

"Later," he said. He made sure I knew our conversation wasn't over.

* * *

I stood beside the bed opposite from my mother and father. Will had said she was almost a skeleton. I couldn't have imagined how anyone could look so gaunt and still be breathing. She was a tall woman, nearly five ten, and she weighed less than ninety pounds. When I put my hand on one of her arms, I felt skin and bone, with nothing between them. The rattle was louder. Each breath forced small bubbles to the edges of her lips.

My father said, "Let's check the tie-down sheet."

We retightened the knots of the rolled-up sheet that stretched across her chest.

My father said, "I'll be back in just a minute."

I must have looked startled because he quickly added, "I'll just be a minute." He took hold of my mother's arm and guided her out the door and into the hall toward the back bedroom. She didn't want to go, but she didn't have the strength to resist him. She tried to protest.

"No, Ernest."

He said, "You need to rest, to sleep."

"I can't do that."

"The doctor said I had to make sure you got to sleep tonight. I'll call you if anything happens."

They got quiet, and then I heard my father say, "You sleep now. Mark will stay with me."

When I heard him tell her that, I remembered the thought I had when he had called to ask me to come home, and I wished I had told him to call me again when it was over. I wished I were in the shoe store sitting on a stool putting a too-tight shoe on a woman's sweaty foot. I wished I were anywhere else.

Grandma jumped. It was like a reflex action—a sudden all-body twitch. I put my hand on her shoulder. Her breathing had changed. Fewer bubbles formed at her lips when she let out a breath. I pulled up the light blanket that covered her so I wouldn't have to touch the cold flesh on her shoulder.

My father returned. He stood across from me and next to a small nightstand. He examined the items on the nightstand—a comb, a brush, a porcelain bowl half filled with water, and a folded washcloth—and seemed to be looking for something. He opened the shallow drawer in the nightstand and picked up a small, maybe a three-inch square piece of mirror glass.

He said, "I'm glad I remembered we had this."

He wiped the mirror with the washcloth and laid it on the nightstand.

"Just in case," he said.

He took a pencil and a small piece of paper from his shirt pocket and put them on the table beside the mirror.

He said, "To mark the time."

The best—the only—way I know how to describe the rest of that night, which went on into the earliest hours of the next morning, is that it kept getting wider and wider. The air in the bedroom was still, the light dim, barely bright enough to see all the way across the small room. The skin around my grandmother's mouth had grown gray and pasty.

My father now and then dampened the washcloth in the basin, wrung it out, and carefully wiped my grandmother's brow. He took the brush and lightly pushed her gray-streaked hair up and back from her face. He fussed with the blanket and rearranged it in the slightest possible way he thought might make her more comfortable. He spoke to her. "There you are" and "That's better" and "It's not so bad, is it?" And he said, "It's all right, Elizabeth. Everything is all right." He brushed away a hair or dried a bead of spittle with a gentleness of touch I had never seen from him before.

*   *   *

My mother came into the room sometime in the middle of the night. She stood beside me.

"How is she?"

My father said, "She's resting."

"She seems quieter."

"She is."

"Do you think it'll happen tonight?"

"Yes, I think so."

The walls of the room could not stop the spreading out of the minutes that followed, minutes that stretched the shadows in the room wider and wider.

My father came around the bed and again took my mother's arm and guided her out of the room.

He said, "Go back to bed. I'll call you."

"You'll be with her? You'll stay? I promised her I wouldn't let her be alone."

"I'll stay."

Shortly after he returned, my father picked up the small piece of mirror and held it out in front of him. He held it delicately, with his thumb and forefinger, the way one might hold the wing of a wounded butterfly, as though he expected the slightest pressure, maybe even the mere thought, of his fingers squeezing the glass any tighter would shatter the mirror into thousands of tiny fragments. He breathed on the mirror and looked at the fog caused by his breath. He wiped it off with the edge of the blanket.

My grandmother let out a breath. He waited. The space between breaths was much longer now. He moved the mirror toward her and held it next to her mouth and nostrils. Wideness covered all. He pulled it away, looked at it, then turned it and showed it to me. I had to lean slightly across the bed to see the light outline of moisture on the bottom part of the mirror. He wiped it off and put it back on the nightstand.

It was not until nearly morning that she finally died. Gray light seeped through the one window in the room. There had been some false alarms, some long spaces waiting for her to breathe, and a few checks with the mirror before he finally held the mirror to her face and pulled it away, only to see in it a clear, unhindered image of himself. He did it twice again—each time his hand trembled a little more, seeming to make light ripples in the air—and he made me look at it too. I do not know exactly when she died. It happened between the last breath and the time she should have taken another one. Like the chicken that had fallen at my feet, there was no time between *she is* and *she was*—no hours or minutes or seconds, even, between *is* and *was* trading places.

I waited through the ever-widening night for it, and I missed it.

The next two days narrowed into a tight, twisting path like the one that goes up the side of the bluffs where Will had fallen. Only instead of eagles' nests, we dealt with arrangements, telephone calls, and visits from friends and from some people we had never met. My father worried about what the funeral was going to cost. My mother worried about who—since my grandmother had not seen the inside of a church in more than twenty years—was going to "say words," as she put it. There were also Will's ankle (a hairline fracture that required a cast) and my job. Added to the mix were the mutterings of my father about how poor the territory had become, and I knew Will was right. He was going to move again.

Two ladies sang "The Old Rugged Cross" and "Life Is Like a Mountain Railroad" at the funeral. I felt sure my grandmother would have preferred a recording of Red Foley singing "Peace in the Valley." The preacher had never met my grandmother, and all of what he had to say about her had come from a short talk with Mother. The preacher talked for about ten minutes and didn't say anything that should have startled anyone. Mother seemed pleased with the way things had been done. She thanked the preacher and the ladies who sang. She clung to the small bouquet of flowers the funeral-home director took off the casket and pressed into her hands.

On the way home, in the back seat of the funeral car, Mother said, "The preacher was good."

My father said, "He talked too long." And he might have said more, but out of the corner of his eye, he caught that quick turn of my mother's head and the way she looked at him. He settled back into his seat and remained silent the rest of the way.

When I woke the next morning, I intended to catch the first available bus. Will was not in his bed, and the house was silent. My clothes were not where I had left them. I found a clean pair of pants and went looking for my mother. She was in the backyard hanging my freshly washed clothes on the clothesline.

She said, "Good morning."

I said, "Good morning. I had hoped to catch an early bus."

She said, "It won't take long for them to dry. It's such a warm day."

It was warm, and a small wind would hurry the drying. I didn't have much choice.

She added, "Your father wants you to help him with some things when he gets back. He took Will to school. There's coffee on the stove."

A big porcelain coffeepot sat in a deep pan almost filled with water over a low flame. I poured a cup and walked through the house to my grandmother's room. I walked into emptiness, a vast hollowness that sucked my breath out of me. The bed linens were gone. A large brown-and-yellow stain covered the middle of the old cotton mattress. I walked around the bed to the nightstand, picked up the small piece of mirror, and looked at myself in it. I breathed on it and wiped off the moisture with my sleeve. I breathed on it again and watched the moisture over my reflection slowly disappear. I was amazed by the fragility of even the sign of life. Maybe I didn't' really think that then, but that's how I remember it.

My mother's footsteps sounded from the kitchen, and I went to meet her.

She said, "I was wondering where you were."

"In the front."

"I'm glad you're still here. I wanted to tell you something before your father gets back. Want more coffee?"

She refilled my cup and poured one for herself and sat at the table. I sat across from her.

She said, "I want to thank you for the other night—for staying up with your father, I mean."

I said, "I was glad to do it." It felt like I had stumbled over the awkwardness of the words. "I don't mean glad. I just mean I thought I ought to."

She pulled a small piece of paper out of her apron pocket and laid it on the table.

She said, "He marked the time." And she smoothed the paper with the heel of her hand.

I looked at the piece of paper. It said "4:47," and I was puzzled. There was no clock in my grandmother's room. Neither my father nor I wore a watch—something about his body chemistry made a wristwatch run fast, and I hadn't been able to afford one yet. And I did not see him write it down. It seemed a strange number.

"It helped him a lot, you being there. He said so. And I don't know what I would have done without him."

My father's car crunched the rocks in the driveway. I don't know where my mother's talk was going, but I was relieved when it was interrupted.

What my father wanted me to help him with was to get rid of the old cotton mattress. We rolled it up and tied it with a piece of clothesline. Then we stuffed it in the trunk of his car the best we could. We used another piece of clothesline to tie down the trunk. Then we carried it to the dump.

On the way there, I said, "I saw the note you made. How did you figure out what time Grandma died?"

"I don't know that I really did. It wasn't daylight yet, so I just guessed. Why? Do you think it matters?"

I said, "No, I guess not. Not really."

I didn't know whether or not I thought it mattered. I wondered if it mattered if he was wrong in a certain direction. *If he gave a few minutes to the record of her life, that would be all right*, I thought. *But what if she had lived longer than 4:47? Would it have been fair to take minutes off her life? That's crazy*, I told myself. And then I asked him if he had decided what he was going to do when Will's school was over.

"Your mother and I are talking about going to Chicago. We can both find work there. It'll be good for your mother to have something to do."

"What about Will?"

"There's bound to be work for him this summer in a city like that. His ankle ought to be all right before we go."

It was definite. He had thought it through, and he had enlisted my mother. The new rainbow rose from the shore of Lake Michigan, and I was more eager than ever to catch my bus to go South.

My clothes were dry by the time we returned from the dump. My mother made me eat a sandwich and pleaded with me to stay, at least until Will got home. That would mean not getting back to Hot Springs until late that night. I wanted to go sooner.

"Tell Will I said goodbye and good luck in Chicago."

She said, "I think he'll like it there."

I heard the doubt in her voice. She saw the doubt on my face and turned away.

My father took me to the bus station. The bus was already there. When we shook hands, he held on an extra moment. He wished me well and said he would stop in to see me next time he was in Hot Springs. He probably would get there at least once before they moved. He thanked me for coming home and for spending that night with him. I got on the bus, took a window seat, and looked for him, but he had already gone to his car. As the bus pulled away, I leaned forward enough to catch a glimpse of him as he drove around the corner, his shoulders hunched over the steering wheel as though he was already halfway to Chicago.

WHEN THE TRUMPET SOUNDS

TWO OF MY grandsons have formed a small band that practices at my house on Saturday afternoons. Because I live alone, it's easier for them here than at their parents' houses, where they're always in the way. In the spring, I like to leave the windows in the house open so I can hear them while I work in my garden. I think they're pretty good. Not ready for the road yet, but who knows about later? If it's their dream and if it isn't, that isn't important. I like to hear them play mainly because they play my kind of music—lots of swing and bebop stuff and newer stuff too. They like Thelonious Monk, and you can hardly go wrong with that. It just takes practice. That's what I tell my across-the-street neighbor, Ferguson.

I know he'll be over soon after they start to play. Most of my neighbors say they like hearing the kids play, but Ferguson is going to complain about them being too loud. I think, secretly, he comes over so he can hear them better. I asked him once what kind of music he likes. I expected him to say Elvis or country. He said that he didn't know much about music and that most of it seemed okay. He figures if something makes it high on the popularity charts, it must be pretty good.

What he actually said was "I like all kinds, so long as it's not too loud."

I'm paying attention to the way my hoe chops off weeds when he comes around the corner of my house. He gets halfway across the backyard before he yells, "Hey, Rambler."

I hear him, but I don't look up. I stay focused on my weeding until he is almost right on me. He hesitates at the end of the row I'm working on. Then when he sees me look up, he walks to meet me and sticks out his hand. I give him mine, and we shake, just like we were being introduced.

It's a gesture that's as ingrained in him as breathing. We've known each other nearly seven years. We've not been what you could call friends, even though we've mostly acted friendly. But for Ferguson, shaking hands with another man was either the bare minimum or the most he needed to do to show he was neighborly.

He says, "Sounds like they play the same number over and over."

"That's what practice is, Ferguson. They do it until they get it right, and then they do it again because they've got it right."

"Does it have to be so loud?"

I say, "They probably could turn it down a bit."

Just at that moment, the kids must have decided they'd had enough of "Satin Doll," and my grandson that plays the electric bass was showing off. He had his amplifier cranked up hard. When he first hit it, Ferguson jumped.

"Goddamn," he says.

I laugh because I know that by the time we could get to the house, the boy would have lowered the volume level so they could start on another tune.

I admit the music is loud, but I do nothing to get it turned down. Ferguson has made his complaint, but he's afraid of complaining too loud and being unneighborly. It's time for him to pretend to take a real interest in my tomatoes then sort of shuffle off home. When the tomatoes are ripe, I'll give him a few, for his wife. This time, I decide to take a different approach.

While he's bent over checking the underside of a tomato for signs of rot, I ask, "Want a glass of lemonade?"

It catches him off guard, and he accidentally snaps the tomato he's examining off the vine. It's still green.

"Sorry," he says.

"How about a cold drink?"

"Yeah, sure, but you got something besides lemonade?"

"I think so. Like a beer?"

Ferguson believes that a Saturday afternoon beer in a neighbor's backyard is a sacrament that cannot honorably be refused. He looks at the open windows that are releasing the sound of a hard-driving tune—it's not one I know—then at me, the house, and me again. He shrugs his shoulders and nods his head.

I say, "There's an ice chest on the patio. Help yourself."

He starts toward the house, then remembers his manners.

"Want me to bring you something?"

"There's a plastic jar with lemonade in it. I'll have some of that."

He says "lemonade." And then he walks to the house, gets his beer and my lemonade, and comes back.

I've moved over to the row of peas, large green bushes with small pods breaking out on them.

He says, "Your peas don't look so good."

"Too much rain, too many bugs."

"You spend a lot of time out here, don't you?"

I think there's nothing like talking about the obvious.

"It's a good place to not have to think."

"Keeps you away from the noise too." He points toward the house.

"I like to think all the music being played has something to do with how my garden grows."

The kids start a new tune, and Ferguson looks back at the house. Before he gets a chance to complain again, I tell him, "That's called 'Song for My Father.'"

Ferguson gets a puzzled look on his face and says, "Does it have words?"

He sees I'm surprised by his question, and he adds, "You said it's a song."

I try to explain that a tune doesn't have to have words to be called a song, but he's not interested in my explanation. He breaks off a couple of underdeveloped pods and examines them. He's already remarked how they don't look good this year, and I can't imagine where the conversation about purple-hulled peas would go from there.

I say, "Let's go sit down. I've done enough here for a while."

We walk over to the lawn chairs under the oak tree. As we walk, Ferguson crumples his empty beer can with one hand. The kids are playing "My Funny Valentine." My oldest grandson is doing the trumpet solo. He's good, although I know he's not as good as I can imagine. Sometimes when I sit in the lawn chair and listen to him play, I get disconnected and have a hard time knowing the difference between what he's really doing and what somebody like Wynton Marsalis could do—the tune climbing on notes so clean and pure they are like connected drops of liquid silver floating upward into the sky. They're the notes I imagine I would have played if I hadn't quit when I was still a kid. Sometimes I can feel the weight of the horn in my hands, and if I close my eyes, I'll see the colors of the tones and feel the shapes they make as they wheel around in bright air, as beautiful as the women who still, now and then, dance naked in my dreams.

Ferguson says, "Hey, Rambler, you going to sit down?"

He has a concerned look on his face, and I realize he's not used to catching an older man in a revery.

I hand him his beer and say, "I'm fine. I was just listening."

The boy is struggling with his breath. He wants to take his solo higher, but his lip doesn't hold. They stop and pick a place to start again.

I say, "He's not quite ready for that one."

Ferguson says, "You used to play something?"

He says it a little too loud, to make a point about the volume of the music coming from the windows.

"A long time ago, when I was a kid. I played the trumpet."

He says, "I guess you outgrew it."

A mockingbird sits on my next-door neighbor's wooden fence and pecks at the soft wood rotting from too many spring rains. The warm afternoon spreads out before us, and Ferguson's remark hovers in the heavy, humid air. I try to ignore it, but the remark has stirred something in me.

"I don't think that's the way I'd put it."

"Do you still play?"

"No," I said. "I used to, when I was a kid. That's been nearly fifty years."

I think about the moment a few weeks before when the boy handed me his horn and told me to try it. I surprised myself by playing a C scale and getting the fingering right, but just that little bit made my lips tingle. I even remembered the first four or five bars of "Blue Moon," but I was glad the boys were the only ones around to hear the tone I got out of the horn. Still, they yelled, "Hey, Grandpa!" And it made me feel good.

"How old were you?"

I must look like I don't understand, because he immediately adds, "When did you quit playing with your horn?"

He makes it sound like something I used to hide in the barn to do, but I let it go and look at the mockingbird on the fence. Ferguson sets his beer can against his crotch and cracks his knuckles.

"I was thirteen."

"How come you quit? Couldn't you play it good?"

I look at him and feel as unneighborly as I ever have. What the hell does he mean drinking my beer, complaining about my grandsons' music, and questioning me about whether or not I played the trumpet *well*?

I say, "That wasn't the problem. My father sold my horn."

"Your old man hocked your horn?"

"He had to pay the light bill. It couldn't be helped."

Ferguson says, "That would have pissed me off. Sounds like something my old man would do. He was an asshole too."

Goddamn you, Ferguson. I think it at least twice, but I don't say it out loud. I know his father—a man less than ten years older than I am with a belly bigger than Ferguson's. He has heavier, darker brows and hands that turn all the way out when they hang at his sides. We tried to have a conversation once, but it was even less successful than the efforts his son and I make at talking about my garden.

Ferguson says, "My grandma bought me a drum once. She's my mother's mother, and I think she did it to get back at my old man for something, figuring the noise might drive him crazy. He wouldn't let me beat it in the house, and my mother put it in the attic to keep me and him from fighting about it. It's probably still there. Once, after I graduated from high school, we was sitting in a duck blind, keeping warm with a bottle of moonshine, and he tried to tell me he was sorry about it. I guess he'd had enough to drink he didn't know for sure what he was saying, because he kept bringing it up and talking about it, until

I got really pissed and told him he could talk till ducks forgot to fly, but I wasn't ever forgetting it. The old fart stumbled all over himself, trying to apologize, and we didn't see a fucking duck all day."

I feel embarrassed, and I can't tell whether his outburst has bothered him or not. He sips his beer and looks away toward the fence where the mockingbird stands guard. A rush of heat fills my chest and spreads upward through my neck into my face and makes my scalp tingle. I can appreciate Ferguson's clumsy attempts at neighborliness at times, or I can at least tolerate them. But not the intimacy of revelations. There are things I don't want to remember. And more than that, there sure as hell are things I will never tell him.

Fifty-two years earlier, my mother went with me the night the salesman came to the school to show the brass horns. My father didn't go; he said he was too busy. And besides, he wanted me to play a clarinet. On long tables set up in the gym, there were trumpets, trombones, tubas, and french horns, and they all looked like they had been dipped in a vat of some maharaja's molten gold. The salesman held a shiny mouthpiece to my lips and told my mother and me how my mouth was *made* for playing the trumpet.

I want Ferguson to go home, but he is ready for another beer. He looks at me from under his brow. He's not going to ask outright for one, but when I nod toward the patio, he gets up and ambles over to the ice chest. He's not more than six feet away from the open window when the drummer starts a ride, does a thing on the snare, and starts working the cymbals until the air is filled with bright metallic sounds.

When he comes back to the chair, Ferguson asks, "What the hell was that?"

"The drummer taking a ride."

"Jesus!"

He sips on his beer and stares at the window. The drummer continues to ride. I admit it's a pretty rough one; he doesn't have it all worked out yet. Right now, it's mostly energy. When he ends, Ferguson shakes his head and lets out a long breath. I expect him to complain again, but instead, he circles back to his interest in my past.

He says, "How long had you been playing when your old man took the horn away from you?"

I ask myself, *Why are you here, Ferguson? What does the universe want from me that demands I put up with this?*

I said, "He didn't take it away from me. It wasn't like that."

He shrugs his shoulders, sips his beer, and says, "How was it?"

2

If I spent my dying breath explaining how it was, I was convinced Ferguson would never understand. It wasn't that it was too complicated, although I was inclined to think that anything more complex than pulling the tab to open another cold beer would have been a reach for Ferguson. It wasn't complicated at all. It was just another event I did not want to remember, another bit of my past that encouraged me to wallow a bit in self-pity. But there was something about Ferguson's tone, about his almost indecent insistence that forced a different perspective. Still, I was convinced there was no point in telling the story to Ferguson.

"How was it?"

It may have been the simplest question anyone has ever asked me, but in the fading light of the afternoon, it loosened a torrent of memories—details of sight and sound, the sensation of swollen lips, the voices of teachers, the half-submerged hopes of seeing my parents in a school concert audience, and the disappointment felt after walking home and finding them sitting by the radio and listening to some quiz show like *Name That Tune.* They never knew when my teacher moved me from the third trumpet section to first chair in the second section. Actually, it was like most other things I did. My parents didn't seem to have much to do with anything. As a result, it never occurred to me that what they did ever made any difference. Not really. Except the moving. That made a difference.

We lived in a small town in Illinois when I started playing the trumpet. Soon after that, we moved to a smaller town in Indiana and, soon again, to another place in Indiana. I practiced my horn, played at school, and I got pretty good. Then we moved again—this time to my grandmother's house in Wichita. It's where we always moved back to when my father was broke, couldn't pay rent, and couldn't find a job he liked or he thought he was suited for. He had a hard time finding work that suited him.

It was my mother's mother's house. It was old, run-down, small, with two bedrooms on one side, a living room and kitchen on the other, and a bathroom in the back. The bedrooms were for the grown-ups. My grandmother slept in the front, with a window that opened onto the front porch. My brother had a pallet on the living room floor, my sister was given the couch, and I slept on a folding wood-and-canvas cot on the front porch. Three huge spirea bushes gave me a little privacy. It wasn't a bad place to sleep in summer, but after school started and the weather began to change, I needed an extra blanket. My father promised to close in the porch before the first freeze.

There was a black upright piano in the living room. A third of the keys had at least some of the ivory chipped off. Sometimes my mother played it, and my father sang; and in order to practice transposing, I played along with them. They played and sang old songs from the twenties and thirties. My grandmother had stacks of that kind of music. They sang and played hymns and spirituals too. One I really liked was called "Steal Away." It was a bluesy spiritual song that had a line in it: "When the trumpet sounds within my soul, / I ain't got long to stay here." I don't know why I liked that line so. It seemed a sad line. But when I got it right, when the horn sang it right, it was also a great line.

Through September and into early October, my father tried to borrow the money he needed to pay for closing in the front porch. Then he lost his job. The nights were already chilly, but I was determined to stay out there as long as I could. There wasn't room for the cot in the living room, and I didn't want to sleep on the floor.

One morning, the cold woke me. I lay on my back and watched my breath. I heard something move and sat up. My father was sitting on the front steps. He was dressed to go looking for work. The collar of his suit coat rode up on his neck and draped off his shoulders like it was a gunny sack thrown across his back. He hunched forward, and I thought he was just cold. My black trumpet case lay across his lap.

I sat up and said, "What's going on?"

He looked straight at me, but I had the feeling he was looking somewhere else—beyond me and at something he had never in his whole life wanted to see. When he spoke, the words came out in a rush, like they were wrapped in the white vapor of his breath hitting the cold air.

"I've got to pay the light bill."

I think I knew what was coming, but I wasn't going to let myself recognize it without it being said.

"I can get twenty dollars for the trumpet at a pawnshop. You understand I'm not selling it. It's like collateral for a loan, and when I get ahead, I'll pay off the loan and get back your horn."

I reached for my shoes under the cot and said, "You paid for it in the first place."

He looked like I had slapped him. I didn't mean to hurt him like that.

My mother came to the door to say my breakfast was ready. I went in past her without looking at my father and the trumpet case cradled in his arms. My mother stayed in the doorway. Although I couldn't see my father clearly, I could tell he was standing on the porch, not close to her and not exactly facing her either. My mother's back was rigid. My father was animated, gesturing as best he could with one hand while holding on to the trumpet case.

Finally, he said it loud enough for me to hear. "Christ, Goldie, what else can I do?"

My mother moved just enough that I could see my father step off the porch. He stood on the sidewalk and looked one way and then the other like he didn't know which way to go. Then he turned and walked toward the bus stop a block away.

He must have gotten the money he needed because the electric company didn't turn off our lights. Nobody in the house said anything about the trumpet. They didn't need to. I understood it was gone forever, and I did my best to avoid the awkward silences that occurred between my father and me. I was determined to let it go, to avoid any kind of scene over it. I might have, too, if there had been more space in the house, or if there had been someplace where I could do homework without hearing their radio.

One of their favorite programs was the Horace Heidt Amateur Hour. I used to daydream about being introduced on the radio as a triple-tonguing trumpet player. Not long after the trumpet was gone, Horace Heidt's voice introduced a trumpeter. When the notes started coming fast and clean, I lost it. I threw my pencil at my books on the kitchen table, stomped through the living room out onto the front porch, and slammed the screen door behind me.

My mother called, "Mark."

My father said, "What the hell?"

My mother said, "Ernest."

My grandmother said, "It's the trumpet."

My father said, "What was I supposed to do?"

My mother said, "Ernest, go talk to him."

When I heard his footsteps, I jumped off the end of the porch and ran. My father called my name, but I kept on running. I knew he wouldn't try to follow me. I knew he didn't want a real confrontation any more than I did. I ran eight or nine blocks until I came to the playground of an elementary school.

The sky over the deserted playground was clear and full of stars. I spun myself on the merry-go-round. Then I sat on a swing and pumped, trying to point my toes straight out at the same star every time. As I swung, I imagined hearing the triple-tongued notes of the trumpeter on the radio. I saw myself on the stage, my trumpet pointing up, the quick, clear notes rising to form new constellations in the cold and distant sky.

I don't know how long I would have swung like that if a pair of Wichita policemen had not stopped and asked what I was doing there. I told them I was just out walking around, thinking about things. I had left without a jacket, and it was cold and getting colder. When they offered me a ride home in their patrol car, I didn't even think about refusing. They didn't hassle me. They just took me home.

In my house, it was as though nothing had happened. I finished my homework—I think it was conjugating Latin verbs—and had a cup of cocoa, which my grandmother fixed for me. The radio was still on but turned down. When it was bedtime, my mother started to put an extra pallet on the floor.

I said, "What are you doing?"

"It's too cold for you to sleep on the porch."

"I don't want to sleep on the floor. I'll take extra covers."

"But it's so cold."

My grandmother came out of her room with a heavy quilt. She handed it to me.

"This will keep you warm."

"Thanks."

My mother started to protest and thought better of it. My father was already in the back bedroom. I didn't know if he was especially tired or if he wanted to avoid me as much as I wanted to avoid him.

I took the quilt and added it to the blankets that were already on my cot. I took off my shoes and put them close under the cot, so I could put them on before I had to put my feet on the floor in the morning.

All the lights—except for my grandmother's bedside lamp—went out. She was a chronic insomniac. Her light would stay on, and her radio would play softly most of the night. My cot was under the window of her room. She always kept it slightly open, even in the coldest weather, because she said she slept better with fresh air. She often put me to sleep with the soft slapping sounds she made putting cards down as she played solitaire on the small table beside her bed.

I don't know what time it was that I awoke and realized my father was sitting in the swing at the far end of the porch. I know it was very late, sometime in the morning, because my grandmother's room was dark. I lay there and watched him watch me, and I wondered whether or not he knew I was awake. The white mist that formed when his breath hit the cold air swirled around the dark shape of his head. Then I moved, turned, and tried to act like my turning was something I did in my sleep, but he knew better.

He said, "Mark, I'm sorry about your trumpet. I want you to know I really do mean to get it back."

I waited what felt like a long time before I said, "Don't worry about it." But I hadn't waited long enough to be able to say it without anger coloring my voice.

He stood and walked past me and went into the house. I lay on the cot and looked at the small strip of sky visible between the roofline and the spirea bushes. The fall constellations turned, and the stars were like notes, the bright sounds of all the trumpets that had ever been played. I had no idea what price my father got for my horn. I never saw it again. We never mentioned it again.

3

"Rambler, hey there. Are you all right, man?"

His voice seems to come from the other side of the yard.

"What's that? All right? Yes, of course. I'm fine."

"Man, it was like you went away somewhere."

"I guess I did, sort of."

The kids start their version of "Night Train." The tenor sax is having a blast, running up and down, going as fast as he can, trying faster than he really can but not stopping for squeaks or missed notes or anything. They're just having fun now, playing loud and brash.

Ferguson has had three beers, and that's enough to allow him to forget how neighborly he wants to be.

"Man, that's too goddamned loud. You gotta do something."

"What do I have to do?"

"Turn it down, Rambler. That's too damned much noise."

"It's not noise, Ferguson. It's music, and they're playing the way they need to play."

I get up and pick up the empty beer cans he has let fall on the grass beside his chair. He looks at me. I think he wants another one, but I'm not going to offer it. I take the empties and throw them in the trash can behind my toolshed. When I come back, he is standing by the ice chest on the patio. I walk over and grab the hoe I had left leaning against the wall. I don't intend to work much more in my garden, but it's the most obvious hint I can think of for Ferguson to leave. He notices it.

He says, "Don't mean to upset you, man, but it's loud."

"That's how it is."

Neither of us offers to shake hands. Ferguson looks again at the ice chest. Then he turns and walks away and disappears around the corner of my house. I don't know why, but at that moment, I believe today is the last day he will come over to complain. He had told me more than I wanted to know, and I had held back what he wanted to know. The kids stop playing, and I lean the hoe back against the house and go inside.

Andrew, the trumpet player, says, "Did Mr. Ferguson give you a hard time?"

"Not really."

The drummer starts to tear down his set.

I say, "Y'all want to practice again tomorrow?"

Andrew says, "Yeah, sure."

"Why don't you just leave your setup the way it is, then?"

Andrew has already put his trumpet in its case, but he hasn't closed the lid. I pick up the horn, insert the mouthpiece, and hold the instrument up in the light. It is golden. I heft it in my hands. Carefully, I wrap my left hand around the valves and bring my right hand up and place my fingertips on top of the valve buttons. I buzz my lips a couple of times. The kids are smiling, but they don't know what to think about me. I bring the horn to my lips and blow. I play a C scale up and back down. My lips tingle, and I hang a little bit on the middle C. Then it's like my fingers somehow, all by themselves, remember how to play the line "The trumpet sounds within my soul." I finish the line and pull the horn down and hand it to Andrew.

I say, "You in a hurry to get home?"

"No."

"Good. Put your stuff away. We need to get to town. You can come too, Kyle."

That's my other grandson.

"Where we going?"

"We're going shopping. You're going to help me find a horn."

"You serious?"

"I'm serious."

To Andrew I say, "You can give me lessons. I'll pay you."

"I don't know how to teach anyone."

"You know more than I do. And if you don't know what to tell me, you can just play and I'll watch. Let's go."

All four of them get excited about the idea, and in a couple of minutes, we're in the van, and I'm backing out of the driveway. Ferguson is in his front yard, trimming his hedge. He looks up. I know he's angry because he doesn't wave. I don't care. I wave at him. The kids wave and laugh.

I drive away slowly so I can watch him trim his hedge. I'm already seeing him in the next week, or two or three, coming out of his house, walking up my driveway, and ringing my doorbell. I'm going to answer the door with a horn in my hand. I don't know what he'll say. I don't care.

I ain't got long to stay here.

And this, Ferguson, this is how it's going to be.

PICKING UP THE PIECES

LAURA PLAYED THE piano. Her fingers followed the notes written in the *Elementary Piano for Adults: Book II*, and the sounds of a Mozart minuet lifted through the open window and down to where I sat on the ground beside the rosebushes. I pulled nut grass from around the Queen Elizabeth—a full, pink rose—and listened to Laura playing the minuet. It was delicate, balanced, ordered. She played about halfway through it, and her fingers stumbled. She started over. She stumbled again, and I heard the sound of the cover closing over the keys. For a moment, I imagined her sitting on the piano bench, looking at, or maybe running her fingers over, the polished wood. I figured she was remembering I had promised nothing would happen to the piano. But she could have been remembering I had made lots of other promises too.

Laura called, "Jason! Jason!"

I called back, "Out here, in the yard."

As soon as I said it, she was standing at the open window, looking out at the yard.

"What time is it?"

I looked at my watch.

"Four thirty and a little bit."

"He's late," she said.

I didn't say anything.

"Where is he?"

"I don't know."

I tried to say it carefully. I didn't want to say it the wrong way. That's how most of our arguments started. I'd say something, anything, and she'd hear something I didn't know I was saying. She said I did the same thing to her sometimes.

I said, "He'll be here."

"He said four o'clock."

"You want to come outside and wait?"

"No." She moved away from the window.

"Ouch," I said.

A dark spot formed on my thumb where I had stuck it on a thorn. Roses are not only beautiful. I stood up and squeezed the wound to make it bleed. My legs were stiff from squatting to pull grass and weeds from the flower beds. I walked from the side of the house that sheltered the roses through the shade of the red oak that stood next to the driveway. A car turned the corner, and I looked to see if it was him. It sped past. The telephone rang in the house, and in a minute, Laura was standing in the window.

"Jason! Jason!" she called.

"Out here," I answered. I stepped away from the tree. She saw me.

"It was him. He called. He said he'd be here in ten minutes."

"OK," I said.

She said, "Do you want me to make some coffee?"

"If you'd like."

"Do you think I should?"

"It's not necessary," I said.

I heard another car turn the corner. It wasn't him, and when I looked back to the house, Laura was gone from the window. The sun angled below the house, and the front yard was all shade. I walked to the end of the driveway and along the street in front of the house. It was not a spectacular house, but it was bigger than any other I had ever lived in. For months after we moved in, I liked to stroll the street at night and see the house in shadows from the streetlamp and see the lights in the windows and hear music—even elementary Mozart—coming through the windows. The sky was clear, and the air was cool with the sun behind the house and with the hint of the first real northern front about to come in and drive the heat back across the swamps and into the Gulf, at least for a little while. I walked in front of the house, looked at it, and tried not to remember the promises I had made about the house too.

Another car turned the corner and moved slowly along the street. There were two men in the car. We were expecting only one, but the passenger pointed toward the mailbox with the name and number GEORGE 1206 stenciled on it. The driver nodded and turned into the driveway. I couldn't tell whether he saw me or not. In a moment, he stood beside his car, and I shook his hand.

"You're Mr. George," he said.

"Yes," I said.

"Arthur Romero," he said.

He was tall and thin. He had dark hair combed straight back and a thin mustache. He wore a short-sleeved sport shirt, open at the collar, and dark slacks, the old-fashioned kind with pleats in the front and a razor crease all the way down to his shoes. They were wingtips, brown and white with the little holes punched in the leather, just like what my grandfather wore for dressing up in the forties. Romero's handshake was firmer than it needed to be, and he held it too long and smiled. I pulled loose from his grip.

Romero pointed across the top of his car and said, "This is my assistant."

A young man—maybe he was twenty—stood on the other side of the car and seemed to be looking at some point ten or twenty feet above my head. I waited for one of them to speak a name, but neither one did.

I said, "Hello."

"Right!" Romero's assistant said.

He stepped toward the front of the car, and I saw that he carried a clipboard with several papers held to it. He was blond, and he wore a Superman T-shirt.

We walked up the driveway toward the carport. Romero and I walked in front, and the young man fell in behind us. We went into the house from the carport, through the utility room, and into the kitchen. I took them in that way because my lawyer had said the auctioneer probably would want to start there. The porcelain coffeepot stood in a pan of water over a low fire on the stove. Laura was not there.

I said, "Excuse me. I'll find my wife."

Neither of them replied, and I went through the house to find Laura. I had supposed she was in the back, in the bedroom or the bathroom. She was not. I came back down the hall and looked in the living room. She was there, sitting in the chair with the cane back and the oak arms that still had a little of the original varnish on them. The chair and a matching sofa were nearly eighty years old, family pieces from Laura's Aunt Emily.

"They're here," I said.

"They?"

"The auctioneer and his assistant."

"Oh," she said.

She ran a finger along the arm of the chair.

"I see you made coffee," I said.

"Yes," she said.

"They're waiting."

"I'm coming. I didn't put out any cups."

"I'll get them," I said.

"Use the blue ones," she said.

"Are you sure?"

"Yes!"

"OK. They're waiting," I said.

"I'll just be a minute," she said.

The auctioneer and his assistant were still standing in the kitchen. Romero leaned with one hand on the table and looked around. I went to the cabinet where Laura kept the cups.

Romero said, "Lived here long?"

I said, "Six years and a little."

"Nice house."

"We like it."

I took four blue cups from the cabinet. They were mugs, and Laura hated them. They were painted a glossy blue on the outside and were white on the inside. The blue was wearing off around the rim. The handle barely had room for a finger. She had always said they were ugly, but she wouldn't throw them away because they had been a gift. I set them in a row on the cabinet and set the spoons and the bowls with the artificial creamer and the sugar beside them. Laura came into the room.

Romero said, "Mrs. George."

He reached out to take her hand, the same way he would if she were another man. She held her right hand to his, and the muscles in her face went rigid at the touch.

"This is my assistant," he said.

The young blond man with the Superman T-shirt grinned. Laura stared at him for a moment, as though she wondered how he had come so suddenly to be there. I realized she had not even seen the assistant until Romero had identified him.

"Well, we might as well get on with it," Romero said.

"Yes. Might as well," I said.

I looked at Laura. She started to say something but stopped and just nodded.

Romero held out a hand toward the assistant. Nothing happened. The assistant was looking out a window into the backyard. Our neighbor's dog was in heat, and she was in our backyard surrounded by a half dozen males. The assistant made a noise, and Romero snapped his fingers twice—*crack, crack!* The assistant jerked away from the window, saw Romero's extended hand, and gave him the clipboard.

"Right!" the assistant said.

Romero took the clipboard and turned toward us. He held it to let us see the paper on top of the several papers held by the clip. It was a legal-size sheet with lines divided into four columns. He pointed to the sheet as he spoke.

"I'm going to make a list of all your possessions that the law says are subject to auction in the bankruptcy."

He looked at us. His face and voice seemed not to have any expression. I got the feeling he was bored with whatever it was he was doing.

He said, "That means I do not list things excluded by the law. We cannot take—"

I felt Laura flinch at *take*. I reached for her arm. I wanted to comfort her, to reassure her. It was going to be all right. She pried at my fingers and removed my hand.

"Dishes, cooking utensils, the stove, refrigerator, or washing machine, although we get the dryer. We don't get children's toys, clothes—except luxury items like a fur coat."

I laughed. The room was getting warm. No one seemed to have heard me.

"Of course, you keep bed linens and other things considered necessary."

Laura said, "What about musical instruments?"

He said, "Whose are they?"

"They're for the children," I said.

Romero asked, "Where are they?"

"At their grandmother's. We thought it would be easier if they weren't here."

He said, "The instruments. Where are they?"

"In different rooms," Laura said.

"So long as they're taking lessons on them, it's all right," Romero said.

I said, "They're taking lessons." And I wondered if I was going to have to prove it.

"They're all right then. If that explains everything, I better get started. I'm going to list things and assign a value to them. The value will be what I believe I can get at the auction. For example, is this the only table and chairs you have?"

I said, "No, there's another set in the dining room."

We maneuvered around the chrome and Formica table in the kitchen toward the extra wide space that opened into the dining room. Romero handed the clipboard back to his assistant and stood in the passageway and looked back and forth at the two tables and sets of chairs. The dining room set was made of wood, with a polished walnut finish and ladder-back chairs.

Romero said, "I usually let folks keep the better one. So I'll call that one table, yellow, twenty dollars, with four matching chairs, five dollars each."

The assistant had produced a ballpoint pen from somewhere and wrote on the paper as Romero talked. They moved back into the kitchen. Romero opened a cabinet door, then another. He turned to Laura.

"You have any electrical things, like blenders or mixers?" he said.

Laura pointed toward a cabinet.

"In there," she said, and she crossed over to the other side of the cabinet area and closed the doors Romero had left open.

The kitchen took less than ten minutes, the utility room hardly five. Laura and I followed them into the den. I was sweating. I listened to Romero's voice as he recited what he saw: television, sofa, chair, recliner, lamps. The inflections never varied. The assistant never responded. He just wrote the quantity, the description, and the appraisal in the proper columns.

I tried to watch Laura. A couple of times, I thought I saw her bottom lip quiver. I wondered if she felt the same emotions I felt when the auctioneer's shapeless voice named objects I had hardly noticed before.

Laura said, "I dripped some fresh coffee just before you came."

Romero turned and said, "Pardon?"

She said, "Would you like some coffee?"

"I would," he said.

"It's in the kitchen."

And we all went back into the kitchen, where the blue cups, the sugar, and the artificial creamer were lined up on the counter. The counter was actually a little bar that extended from the wall and divided the working area from the table area. There were four high stools, which Romero had listed, against the counter, but Romero ignored them and stood. The assistant pulled one of the stools toward him until he looked up at Romero's face. He replaced the stool against the counter and stood beside the auctioneer.

Laura poured the coffee. Her hand trembled, but she avoided spilling. The assistant put mounds of sugar and creamer in his coffee.

Romero took just a little sugar and sipped. Laura fixed hers and held her cup in both hands. I drank mine black, and I burned my tongue.

Romero said, "What happened?"

I looked at him. I looked at Laura. I didn't know whether he was talking to her or to me.

"Wasn't there enough business?"

He was talking to me. He wanted to know what happened. I felt the bitterness I had been fighting for months, and a sour taste swelled in my mouth. I almost asked if he wanted the explanation of how I, or we went bankrupt in twenty-five words or less. *He* wanted to know what happened. *I* wanted to know what happened. I *knew* what happened. Bad management. Mine. Desperation. Good money after bad. Mine and the bank's. My ears rang. I felt flushed.

I said, "Too many mistakes."

My voice came from a distance, like a voice spreading out across water. I looked at the assistant in the Superman T-shirt and wondered if he had ever tried to fly. I would have bet he had. I heard Romero's voice coming back across the water.

"Too bad," he said.

I agreed with him. He sipped his coffee and seemed to study his cup. He looked at Laura.

"A pretty cup," he said.

"That's all that's left, those four," she said.

"There were eight," I said.

"They were a gift," she said.

Romero sipped again. The assistant took a couple of large swallows, emptied his cup, set it on the counter, and said, "Right!"

Romero said "a pretty cup" and set his on the counter.

It was an ugly cup. Its finger hole wasn't big enough. The blue was too glossy and worn off around the rim. Ugly.

"Guess we should finish," Romero said.

Laura took the cups and put them in the sink. I led the way through the den and down the hall to the bedrooms. Laura did not follow. Romero and his assistant went quickly through the children's bedrooms, listing almost nothing. In our bedroom, there were only a couple of lamps and an occasional table that he listed. I looked for Laura as we went from room to room, and I figured she was cleaning up the coffee things. But how long did it take to wash four ugly blue cups?

Romero said, "Is this all there is?"

I said, "No. There's still the living room."

I wanted to be thorough. The lawyers had warned us to be thorough, to make certain we did not seem to be hiding anything. We could get in a lot of trouble if *they* thought we were hiding anything.

Laura was in the living room. She sat in the center of her Aunt Emily's sofa and put her hands out to the cushions on either side of her. She was not doing a very good job at hiding her anger. It shone in her eyes and reddened her face. It made the muscles on the sides of her neck taut and bulging. I had the impulse to touch her. I suppose I was thinking I could calm her. I knew better and kept my hands to myself.

Romero and his assistant moved to the center of the room and looked around. The auctioneer bent over the cane-back chair and stroked the wood. It was a caress—the touch of a lover who has at last found a value he has been searching for.

He said, "This is old."

I said, "It was her aunt's."

"How old is it?"

"I don't really know."

I thought he didn't believe me, but I told the truth, in a sense. I didn't know exactly when Aunt Emily had bought the sofa and the chair. And I didn't know whether my saying they we were *about* eighty years old would increase or decrease their value in the auctioneer's eyes.

Laura said, "Mr. Romero."

He said, "Ma'am?"

I saw it coming. I wanted somehow to reach out and grab her words with my hands and keep them from escaping into the room.

She said, "I want to tell you this set once belonged to my aunt. It isn't very elegant, but it—and that piano—mean more to me than anything else I could own. I don't want to lose them."

The auctioneer said, "Talk to your husband, ma'am. He's the one went bankrupt."

There was thunder in the room, thunder and cymbals crashing and heat making sweat pop out on my forehead, and a whirling sensation. Inside my head, I heard someone scream "SON OF A BITCH," and it took some time to get started again. When time did start again, I realized I was the only one who heard the thunder and the scream. I could not look at Laura. I looked at her Aunt Emily's sofa, chair, and the piano at the other end of the room, and I remembered how many times I had heard her struggle through the little Mozart minuet before she ever got it right. I felt ashamed.

Laura said, "The lawyer told us we would have first chance to buy our things back. Is that right?"

Romero said, "Yes, ma'am. Most of your furniture won't bring much at an auction, and if you can come up with the cash and save us the trouble of having to haul your stuff out of here, I can arrange for you to keep everything."

I said, "How much money?"

He said, "I don't know. I'll have to add it up first."

He turned back to his work, and it was soon over. I heard little else but the shapelessness of his voice as he recited items and numbers. He finished in the living room, went outside, and listed the garden and lawn tools in the storage shed. I followed him. Laura did not. It took him only a few minutes to finish his counting and listing to come meet me on the carport.

He held out a clipboard and a pen for me to take.

He said, "Look it over and sign at the bottom."

"What's this?"

"It's your inventory. I'll assign values to each item, add them up, and tell you how much cash you'll need to keep what you want. You'll hear from me in a day or two. It won't be hard to do. You don't have much."

I grabbed the clipboard and jerked it out of his hands. The pen fell to the ground. Damned if I would pick it up. He took another pen out of his shirt pocket. I took it, signed at the bottom of the page on the clipboard, and handed it back to him.

"Is that it?"

"That's it."

I realized I was still holding the pen he had handed me. I held it out. He bent over and picked up the pen that had fallen on the carport, put it in his pocket, and began to walk toward his car. I followed him.

I said, "How much time will we have to raise the cash?"

He said, "A week, maybe ten days. It's negotiable, if you really think you can get it."

I didn't tell him a friend had already offered the money.

I said, "We'll get it."

We walked to the car, and Romero stopped and looked around again. His eyes went all the way up to the roofline of the house—I wondered if he worked for the bank too—and down and across to the ground and the rosebushes on the other side of the yard.

"Nice roses," he said.

"Thanks," I said.

He offered his hand, and I shook it. It was sticky with sweat.

The assistant looked at me over the top of the car and said, "Right."

In a moment, the auctioneer and the young man in the Superman T-shirt had gone, and I stood in the driveway and sucked at the pain in the dark spot on my thumb. I didn't want to go back into the house filled with bankrupted promises. Laura was in there. I spent an hour pulling nut weed.

When I went back to the house, I found Laura in the kitchen standing by the counter with the blue cups in her hands.

She said, "He thought these were pretty."

"He did say that."

She said, "They're ugly. Really, look at them."

The cups fell from her hands and crashed on the floor. Pieces of broken blue and white glass spread out in no kind of pattern at all. She said, "He shouldn't have said that."

"What's that?"

"He shouldn't have blamed you."

"Oh, *that*," I said.

I shrugged and made a gesture with my hand to show how easily I had blown it off. Neither of us believed either the shrug or the gesture.

"It doesn't matter," I said.

I moved toward her, and the fragments of glass crunched under my feet.

She said, "I wish I hadn't served them any coffee."

I said, "I'm glad you did."

"Why?"

"Because otherwise, you might never have broken these ugly cups."

"I always thought they were ugly," she said.

"Ugliest cups ever made," I said.

"You noticed? You really noticed?"

"I never knew why you kept them."

We knelt down, surrounded by fragments of blue and white glass, and began picking up the pieces. Laura worked carefully but swiftly. I held the dustpan as she finished sweeping the smallest pieces of glass. When she finished, I stood and looked at her. She held up the broom and smiled as she took the dustpan from me. She deposited the shards of glass in the trash can under the sink. I thought I heard her say something.

"What's that?

She said, "That's it."

I was puzzled. We had filed for bankruptcy. We could expect some difficult times ahead. Still she smiled.

"Why are you smiling?"

"I've been wanting to get rid of those cups for a long time. That awful man doesn't know he did us a favor."

A BOY IN THE WOODS

A SMALL BOY walked along a path deep in the thick woods that bordered a large lake. Bright sunshine filtered through the thick canopy of branches and leaves that made large areas of deep shade. The underbrush had not been cleared in years, and a thick layer of dead leaves covered the path. The boy shuffled his feet and kicked at the leaves, stirring up clouds of dust and the sharp odor of leaf mold and decay.

The boy was ten years old. He wore faded and dirty blue jeans and a polo shirt with broad horizontal stripes. A cowlick made his straight brown hair fall constantly in his face. He had fine, almost delicate, features. He was thin, small-boned, with dark-brown eyes that looked down or away whenever an adult asked him a question.

A man followed a few feet behind the boy. Every few steps, the boy made quick glances over his shoulder. The man smiled when the boy turned to look at him. After they walked on for a few minutes, the boy noticed movement in a pile of leaves a few feet off the path. He stopped and held up his hand to motion for the man to stand still.

The man asked, "What's the matter?"

The boy put a finger to his lips and pointed at a squirrel sitting up on its haunches in the leaves.

The man said, "It's just a squirrel," and he started to urge the boy to go on.

The boy said, "Don't move."

The man obeyed. The boy took a deep breath. The squirrel cocked its head and looked straight at the boy. The boy let out a slow breath as he slowly picked up a foot, as if he was practicing moving in slow motion, and took a step toward the squirrel. Then he stopped. He took another deep breath and held it for a moment before he decided to take another step toward the squirrel.

When the boy lifted his foot to make another step, the squirrel turned and darted up a large tree. It stopped on the trunk, high enough to be out of reach, and turned its head almost completely around. Then it climbed a couple of feet higher and looked again toward the boy before it disappeared in a thickness of branches and leaves. The boy wanted to climb the tree after the squirrel.

The man put a hand on the boy's shoulder and said, "Come on."

"Wait."

"You won't catch it."

The man turned the boy and pushed on his back.

"Come on. My car's just a little ways up the path. I told you I would take you home."

The man put his arm around the boy's shoulder and pulled the boy close to his side. The boy pulled back, and the man laughed and released him.

The boy asked, "What time is it?"

"Almost four."

The boy looked at him, disbelieving. The man showed him his watch and added, "I wouldn't lie to you."

"I have to get home before my father does."

His father had told him to stay out of the woods. He had told the boy a story about a child's body being found in the woods, all covered up with dry brown leaves and fallen branches. Terrible things had happened to the boy, he had said, and it was too terrible to explain what they were. He had told the story as though it was something that happened recently, but the boy thought it had to have been a long time ago, because he did not remember its happening.

The boy said, "I have to hurry."

"Then leave the squirrel alone."

The man pushed lightly on the boy's back between his shoulder blades and urged him to walk on. They came to a fork in the path, and the man used only a slight pressure to turn the boy down the one that went to the left, away from the lake. In a few minutes, the boy saw the man's car—a black Ford coupé—standing in a small clearing.

"Race you," the man said and started to run, grabbing the boy's arm to pull him along. The boy tripped on a tree root and fell. His hip landed on a piece of broken limb hidden under the leaves. He cried out, and the man turned to help him up.

"Are you all right?"

"I'm fine." He fought back tears.

"Sure you are."

The man led the boy toward the car and opened the passenger-side door. "I better look at that."

"It's all right."

"You might have cut yourself."

"I didn't."

The man smiled. "I better make sure."

The man bent forward and reached for the buckle on the boy's belt. He easily overcame the weak resistance of the boy's hands pushing against him. He undid the belt, worked the jeans and undershorts down to the boy's knees, and put his hand on the boy's hip.

"It's not cut," the man said and moved his hand around to touch the boy's genitals. "It's getting big. You must be playing with it."

The boy blurted, "No I'm not."

The boy looked down at himself and wondered if the man could really tell that sometimes he played with himself. The man laughed, reached up, and messed up the boy's hair.

The boy reached down to pull up his jeans. The man stopped him, stood him up, and turned him toward the car until the boy lay bent over with his face against the seat cushion. The boy tried to stand, but the man pressed his hand against the boy's back between his shoulder blades and held him firmly against the seat.

"Hold still," the man said.

Branches and leaves deflected sunlight through the windshield, and dust motes pirouetted in the bright air. The smells of dust, of stirred leaves, of dead wood, and of stagnant water from the lake tickled and burned the boy's nostrils. Sunlight and flickering shadows of leaves filled the space in front of his eyes, and the rough texture of the seat upholstery scratched his face. He felt some weight on his back, and a sharp pain cut through him, like a knife running up his spine to the base of his skull. He gasped for air, and his hands clawed the seat cushions.

In a moment, the pain became something dull that pushed his face harder into the seat. The weight on his back got heavier, and the car moved beneath him—first slow, then faster, rhythmic, like his rapid heart, like the dusty breath of the woods filling his lungs until he was sure they would burst.

He closed his eyes and made himself rise up through the roof of the car, beyond the trees, beyond the bright sky, past the clouds, past the sun, into a whirling darkness that was so deep it had to be the place where the silence of the woods came from. The darkness had a heart, and he felt it beating. He could neither see it nor hear it, but he felt it. It was not his heart, but it felt like it could have been. Then the car stopped moving, and the weight lifted itself off him.

"Stand up."

The man pulled on the boy's shoulder and helped him stand. He held out a rag to the boy.

"Go over there in the bushes and take a dump. Use this to wipe yourself."

The boy took the rag and hobbled with his jeans and shorts pulled halfway up his legs. Something sticky wet the crack between his buttocks.

"Hurry up. I want to get you home before your daddy gets there. I wouldn't want you to get in trouble."

The boy did not speak during the ride home. When the man reached over and patted his knee, he squirmed and pulled himself as tightly against the door as he could.

The man said, in a comfortable, offhand way, "You know you can't tell anyone, don't you?"

The boy did not answer.

"Don't you?" The man's voice, for the first time, sounded menacing. "Something really bad might happen if you tell anyone. It would be sad if your father got hurt real bad someway because you told a story nobody would believe. You understand, don't you?"

The boy nodded and leaned his head out the window and let the wind strike him full in the face. The wind made his eyes burn, but he kept his face turned out to catch the wind until the car stopped in front of his house.

When the man stopped the car, he put his hand in his pocket and pulled out a quarter. He tried to hand it to the boy.

"Here. Take it."

The boy looked at the coin held in the man's fingers and shook his head.

"Take it."

"No."

The man looked up at the house and saw the boy's sister, older by two years, sitting in the porch swing. He put the coin back in his pocket.

The boy said, "I have to go."

"You know you can't tell, don't you? I mean nobody. You understand that? Nobody."

"Yes."

The man made a fist and lightly punched the boy's arm.

"Good boy."

The boy got out of the car and ran up to the front porch.

His sister said, "Don't worry. Daddy's not home yet. You're safe."

* * *

The clock on the wall over the kitchen stove said it was just after five. His mother moved about the kitchen, preparing supper, and nearly bumped into him with a pot of hot food she had just lifted off the stove.

"Supper won't be ready until your father gets home. Go do something until I call you."

As he turned to go, she said, "Wait."

She put the pot back on the stove then reached and pulled at something in his hair. She handed him a piece of a leaf.

"Where did this come from?"

"I fell in the backyard."

Even such a small lie made his face redden. He looked at his feet. If his mother noticed, she didn't say anything. She just held out the leaf for him to take.

"Throw this in the trash or take it outside. I don't need to be sweeping up dead leaves in my kitchen. Go on."

He went out into the backyard and tossed the leaf into the air so he could see which way the wind was blowing. It was something he had seen Tonto do in a movie. There was no wind. The leaf spun slowly to the ground, and he put his shoe on it and ground it until all that was left was dust.

The yard was small, not big enough for playing any kind of game. An old green apple tree grew near the back fence. The apples were not good for eating raw—cooking apples, his mother called them—but the tree had low branches that made for easy climbing. He pulled himself up and climbed well up into the tree. The foliage was thick, and the green apples were only beginning to fall. He liked sitting in the shadows of the leaves and branches and watching his mother through the kitchen window.

A sound turned him to look toward the elm tree that had thick dark branches up high, hanging over the roof of the house. A blur of brown leaped from the elm onto the roof and somehow came off the eave, turned itself upside down, and disappeared into an air vent. His father was supposed to have repaired the screens on those vents weeks before to keep the squirrels from getting into the attic. If his mother heard the squirrel in the attic, she would start fussing at his father again until he promised to get that hole stopped up, even though he knew it wouldn't do any good. Nobody could keep that squirrel out of anywhere it wanted to go.

After a while, the boy's mother called him in for supper. His father and sister were already seated at the table. His mother waited for him to be seated. Then she sat and bowed her head. Anyone looking through a window might have admired the scene: the family of four, their heads bowed at grace, a small bouquet of cut flowers in the center of the table. It could have been the perfect subject for a Norman Rockwell cover on the *Saturday Evening Post*.

The boy's father asked him, "What did you do today?"

"Nothing."

"Where did you do it?"

"Out by the lake."

The boy choked on his own words. He hadn't meant to tell his father he had gone to the lake, but his father only looked at him and smiled.

"I thought your bike has a flat tire."

"I walked."

"That's a good ways to walk, hot as it is."

Depending on which part of town one lived in, the farthest distance to the lake was a little more than a mile and a half, and it was not uncommon back then, in that safer time, for boys to walk to it.

"How did you get home?"

The boy swallowed hard, took a drink from the glass of milk by his plate, and looked down at his hands in his lap.

"How did you get home?"

The boy was afraid to say who had brought him home and was afraid his father might guess something about him being with the man. He looked at his sister. She had seen him come home in the man's car, and the boy didn't know whether she would blurt it out if he didn't tell.

He said, "I got a ride," and he stopped.

His father waited a moment then asked, "Who with?"

The boy told him, and his father looked at his mother and again at the boy for a long moment before he said, "Don't go getting into cars with anyone we don't know."

The boy knew his father had met the man at a burial service for a local—a marine who had been killed on some island in the Pacific. The man had shown up in his navy uniform to help carry the casket. After the funeral, the boy's father had lined up with other men of the town to shake hands with the pallbearers and to thank them for being so upstanding. His father had said the pallbearers were all good men because they had fought in the war.

His mother said, "I baked a pie. Anybody want some?"

Without waiting for an answer, she got up and went into the kitchen.

The boy's father said, "Did you go into the woods?"

"Just a little ways."

He didn't hesitate to answer. He had already given up the fact that he had gone to the lake, and anybody would know that it was almost impossible to go to the lake without going at least a little way into the woods.

"You remember what I told you about that, don't you?"

"Yes, sir."

"You're not old enough to remember, but a child got murdered in there once."

The boy couldn't think of a way to respond to his father's remark. He didn't want to tell his father. He had begun to wonder if it was true. He had asked friends at school about the story, but none of them could remember a child being murdered in the woods.

He became uncomfortable in the silence, and if only to hear his own voice, he said, "I almost caught a squirrel."

His mother came into the room with the pie and plates and set them on the table.

She said, "You leave those animals alone. Some of them have rabies."

His sister said, "He thinks he's a squirrel. He's always up in that tree. Looks like one too."

Before he could answer, his mother said, "Stop it." She glared the boy and his sister into silence. Then she turned to the father.

"Since we're on the subject, when exactly are you going to plug up that hole I told you about? The sound of those squirrels running back and forth in the attic woke me up at three o'clock this morning."

His father said, "Saturday."

"That's what you said last week."

"Dammit, I'll do it this Saturday."

That exchange between his parents took away any attention being paid to the boy, and he used the opportunity to finish his dessert and ask to be excused from the table.

Gray twilight spread through the summer night sky. He went out and looked for Venus. He knew it was always the first star to be seen at night. His teacher had told him it wasn't really a star; it was a planet. He liked finding it in the evening, but he almost never got up early enough to see it in the morning.

As the sky darkened, he chased fireflies and put them in a glass jar with a lid he had punched holes in to let the fireflies have air. He always let them go. He played hide-and-go-seek with a half dozen other kids from the neighborhood. He had become really clever at hiding. He was almost always the last one to be found. Sometimes he would stay hidden until the others were forced to give up and quit the game. And sometimes he kept himself hidden away until his mother came out on the porch and called for him to come in. He could not have told anyone why, but those were the best nights.

After his bath, his parents allowed him to go to his room and read for another half hour while they stayed in the living room and listened to the radio. He read a story about Frank Merriwell, the most extraordinary athlete in every sport he had ever heard of. The boy was, in fact, an avid reader—a trait that, more than a few times, had often prompted his father to ask if it was healthy for him to read so much. A teacher asked the class once what their parents read at home, and it hurt him to answer he didn't think they read anything, except maybe the Sunday newspaper.

He heard the radio go silent, and he knew what was coming next. His mother came into the room, waited for him to finish the page, took the book, and laid it on a shelf on the other side of the room.

She said, "It's bedtime. Get ready. I'll come back in a little bit." As she left the room, she added, "Don't forget to brush your teeth."

He undressed and put on his pajamas in the bathroom. He didn't forget to brush his teeth, but he avoided looking in the mirror over the sink. It was because he was afraid he might see a mark on his skin or an unnatural speck in the color of his eyes—a sign that would tell the world the secret he was never to tell anyone. Never—not ever if he didn't want his father to get hurt. His boy mind thought that if he didn't look, it wouldn't be there; but if he looked and he saw it, then he believed that everyone could see it.

When he had been in the bed a few minutes, his mother returned, and he watched her as she came near the bed. He didn't even need the thin sheet he had pulled up over him, but he clung tightly to its edge in a way that would make it easy for him to pull it over his head in case she leaned over to kiss him. She acted as though she didn't notice. Earlier that same summer, she had stopped kissing him good night after several instances of him obviously turning away, trying to avoid the kiss. She thought he was acting out his little boy's skewed perception of maleness.

Truth was, tonight, he feared that if she came too close to him—if she touched him with her lips or if he let her look too closely in his eyes—she might know. She often confounded him by knowing what he had done, where he had been, or what he had said when he believed it wasn't possible. At times, he thought she knew everything, and the fear squeezed his chest until he had to gasp for breath. That fear multiplied itself like stars growing in the sky when she turned out his light.

As she closed his door, she said, "Sweet dreams."

He lay in the dark and listened to the soft sounds the house made at night. He could barely hear music from the radio in his parents' bedroom and the soft murmur of their voices. He looked at the ceiling and thought he heard the rapid patter of the squirrels running in the attic. He wished he had x-ray vision so he could see through the ceiling and the dark. He wished he could live with them in the attic, and he fell asleep thinking about the squirrels.

He dreamed about being in the woods by himself, and he was frightened. He seemed alone, but he knew someone was looking for him. He followed one path after another, constantly turning his head and looking over his shoulder. Every few steps, he stopped and listened, but he heard absolutely nothing. Here and there, he caught movement in the corner of his eye, but when he turned toward it, there was only the woods—thick, heavy trees and deep underbrush—and the acrid smell of dust and mildew and rot.

He went on until he came into a large clearing. Squirrels chattered in a tree above him. Leaves rustled with the movement of squirrels running along the branches. A brown head popped out and disappeared. A brown tail stuck through the leaves. Small, beady eyes, then more eyes and more eyes all the time glistened in the tiny spaces between leaves as high up as he could see.

A large fallen tree lay across the clearing, and he sat on it so that he looked directly at the hugest tree he had ever seen. As soon as he sat, a squirrel ran down the trunk of the tree, headed straight for a pile of dead leaves. It stopped, looked around, pushed its head into the leaves, and came back out with something in its mouth. It sat up and looked around again, this way and that way—the way the boy sometimes did when he wanted to sneak past an open door that led to a room full of adults.

The boy held himself perfectly still. The squirrel ran a few feet back toward the big tree, stopped, swiveled its head to look around the clearing, and looked straight at the boy. Both the boy and the squirrel held their breath, and the boy felt the squirrel's eyes lock on to his.

What did it know? What did it see? Was there something he couldn't see that was visible to others? Was there something about the way he walked? Would older boys make jokes about him being bowlegged, saying his legs were pleasure-bent the way they said it about some girls?

Another squirrel came down the tree, then another and another until brown and gray squirrels filled the clearing. Each one seemed to take its turn to run in front of the boy, stop, look at him, nod its head, and yield its place to yet another squirrel. This went on until all the squirrels had taken their turn. Then they ran in a steady flow of five, six, or seven at a time, up the big tree to hide in all the branches and leaves.

The last two squirrels stopped halfway up the trunk and looked back at the boy. One of them waved its tail excitedly and chattered in a way that made the boy think it was asking him to come closer.

A man's voice shouted somewhere in the woods, and the boy jumped up and ran toward the tree. The pair of squirrels moved down toward him but stayed half an arm's length out of reach. They started a rapid chatter then ran up the tree a ways, stopped, looked back at the boy, chattered some more, and ran up a little farther. He stepped closer to the tree, stretched his arms upward, and felt himself being lifted into the canopy of the leaves and branches of the tree. And he understood what the chattering choir was telling him: "Hide, little squirrel, hide."

When the boy woke, sweat had made his pajamas stick to his skin. The images of the dream clung to his mind as though they were right behind his eyes, and it took him a few seconds to realize just where he was. Gray light seeped through the blind on his bedroom window, and he watched it slowly brighten. He heard the sounds of others moving around, the sound of water flowing from a tap, and the sound of his parents' radio being turned up. He tried hard to hold on to the last fragments of the dream. For a moment—hardly that—it seemed he heard the chatter of the squirrels, but it all disappeared when his mother stuck her head in the room and told him to get up and get dressed.

He got up, took off his pajamas, and put on clean underwear, pants, shirt, socks, and shoes. He went into the bathroom and relieved himself. Then he brushed his teeth, avoiding the mirror. Then he went to the kitchen, where his parents sat drinking coffee at the table.

His father said, "Looks like you're ready for another day."

His mother said, "Did you make your bed?"

His father said, "Remember what I said about those woods. You stay out of there."

"Yes, sir."

His mother said, "The bed."

After he made his bed and ate a bowl of cereal—and after his father had gone to work and while his mother gathered clothes to put in the wash—he went outside and climbed the apple tree and watched for the squirrels to come out of the attic vent and jump onto the long dark branch of the elm.

The boy sat in the tree and felt the day get warmer. He felt the weight of muggy air as he watched for the squirrels. Quick brown movement caught his eye, and he saw a squirrel come from the vent. The squirrel did its upside-down trick to get onto the roof and run for the elm tree. The boy watched it leap onto the branch, leap again onto a lower branch, and disappear in the foliage. A second one followed, and the boy could hear them chattering, invisible behind the leaves.

The boy closed his eyes and strained to understand what the squirrels might be saying. He wished he could climb higher in the apple tree and leap the wide distance to the larger elm. He wanted—more than he would ever want anything else in his whole life—to be a squirrel and to live safely hidden by the leaves of the elm forever.

THAT SUMMER DAY

THE FIRST GRAY hour of morning when shadows emerged from the receding darkness was the only perfect hour of the day. Nothing had happened yet. The day was all promise, all possibility. That was the way it was the last morning I sneaked out the back door and ran across the yard to safety behind the wash shed. I put on the shoes I had carried out of the house and waited, listening for sounds of anyone inside accidentally being awake. But there was nothing. After a short while, I looked around the corner of the shed at the blurred, silent house, still a shadow in the gray dawn.

There were still no signs of wakefulness in the house, but to make sure I wouldn't be caught, I climbed the fence behind the shed, went through the vacant lot behind our yard, and finally reached Center Street. Then it didn't matter if anyone awoke—I was away. Nearly all the houses I passed were quiet and dark like our house, and even those that showed signs of life seemed blurred in the morning's near light.

I was alone on the street except for a handful of old people walking slowly on their way to early Mass. The town was even more deserted than it was late at night, when life could be detected in the shadows of inadequate streetlamps. At night, sounds of music and laughter from Gary's Bar carried through my opened bedroom window. The night town was loud, with an aggregate sound like the unmelodic whistle of someone walking past the cemetery in the dark. But the morning town was quiet, and it seemed confident with no need for a heroic whistle.

I turned onto Church Street and walked to the edge of town where the street narrowed into a dirt road leading only to the Chauvin farm three miles away. I followed the road for a little more than a mile, walking between late-summer brown fields stretching away on both sides of the dry, narrow lane of dust. The gray early light exploded into the blinding glare of the new sun, and it was day in the country. Soon I saw the wood that surrounded Mr. Chauvin's pond, and I left the road and walked across the empty field toward the shade and the cool water.

The wood was thick with pecan trees, the remains of a fig orchard, and sweet olives. And towering above all of them was an ancient live oak, its low-arching branches spread to shade a good third of the pond. Long before I had even heard of it, Mr. Chauvin had made the pond. It was unusually large in both breadth and depth, and it was unusually clean, except on one side where stumps and debris were hidden under the water. One old pecan tree stuck out of the water about twenty feet from the bank and marked the edge of the uncleared area. The rest of the tree was fallen but still precariously attached to the stump, and it formed a bridge from the stump to the bank. The pond had been stocked once, and there was a clear area on the bank where men had sat to fish. But it had been years since anyone had tried to catch fish there. For as long as I could remember, it had served only as a swimming place for the boys from town; but even then, they mostly quit coming when the pool was built in Jeanerette, only two miles away. Throughout that summer, I hadn't met anyone during the early hours I went to the pond.

The sun was high enough to shine through the breaks in the trees, forming a stenciled patchwork of shadow and light decorated by the grillwork of limp-hanging Spanish moss. I undressed and placed my clothes beneath the oak and splashed into the water. I floated on my back with the sun now and then reaching me, warm on my face. I thought of my father having to go to work; but most of the time, I just swam and thought of nothing except how cool the water felt. I took a deep breath and swam underwater as far as I could. When I surfaced, a floating twig bumped my shoulder; and for an instant, I thought it was a snake. I imagined finding a big moccasin and killing it. I practiced my butterfly stroke. I remembered my mother's countless unheeded warnings about swimming alone. I thought perhaps another person would appear to go swimming, and I would have to save someone from drowning. The town would make me a hero. My picture would be in the Jeanerette paper, and I probably would be made chief altar boy for at least a month.

I swam back to the bank where my clothes were heaped, dried myself with my T-shirt, and got dressed. I sat under the oak and watched the outer edge of the shadow of its elegant moss-draped branches recede as the sun rose higher in the sky. When the edge of the shadow reached the old pecan stump, it would be time to start for home. I had at least a couple of hours before I would have to leave.

"Hello. What are you doing?"

The girl's voice came from behind me and startled me, so I jumped and turned around and almost fell into the pond. The girl who had spoken was about the same age as my older sister—maybe around sixteen or seventeen. I looked at her, and she smiled as though she knew she had done something no one else could have by catching me in what I thought was my private hiding place.

"What's the matter? Can't you talk?" she asked.

She laughed, and I felt funny. I knew my face had reddened and my eyes were even misty, so for a moment, she looked almost unreal where she stood, sort of half-leaning against the tree. I couldn't meet her look for long. I looked down at my shoes and watched a platoon of ants string out in front of my feet. It was strange. After many times wishing I would find someone with whom I could share the pond, now that someone had appeared, I had no words for her. No doubt I would have known what to say to any of the boys from town. But in front of this girl—a girl I had never met before—I was, for a few moments that seemed like the whole morning, unable to speak. I kicked the damp earth of the bank and watched the ants scurry as though they were an army overcome by a giant and forced into the chaos of retreat.

Finally, I looked up and said, "Of course I can talk. What are you doing here?"

She laughed. "No fair. I asked you first. You act like you never saw a girl. Do you care if I use your pond and shady spot too?"

"It isn't my pond. It belongs to Mr. Chauvin."

She laughed again. It was a strange laugh. It wasn't like the silly giggle my sister always interjected whenever I tried to talk to her. I couldn't tell whether the girl was only slightly amused at my embarrassment or took unusual delight in my inability to make sense. She stood away from the tree, walked around, and sat where I had been only a few minutes before. She looked out at the quiet pond. There were no sounds except my breathing and the blood pounding at my head. She looked at me again.

"Sit down. You look funny standing up there, hopping from one foot to the other."

I felt the flush come back into my cheeks, and I became confused as she started to laugh again. On the other side of the little clearing, there was an old rotted limb that had been knocked to the ground by lightning. I sat on it. It was quiet again for a while, and then I found the courage to ask, "What's your name?"

"Emma. Emma Chauvin. My uncle owns this pond. I've a mind to tell him about you. I bet he doesn't know you come here alone."

She laughed again, and again there was something cold and strange about her laugh and about the way she tried to make me uncomfortable. I decided not to like her, and I wished she had never appeared. For a moment, I was afraid she might be staying the rest of the summer and my private excursions to the pond would be ended. I broke off a piece of one of the dead limb's smaller branches and used it to draw meaningless figures in the dirt.

"Don't worry. I won't tell on you. Do you come here often?"

Without looking up and without knowing why I bothered, I mumbled an answer. "Nearly every morning, if I can get away before everybody else gets up."

"I bet your momma would be mad if she knew you were here, wouldn't she? I think I'll go to town this afternoon and tell her. Where do you live?"

"It wouldn't do any good. She knows I come here. She's glad to have me out from underfoot."

When she laughed again, I tried to ignore her, but I glanced every now and then to see if she was looking at me. She was prettier than my sister. Her hair was brown and soft and long, reaching past her shoulders, and she had the deepest and darkest eyes I had ever seen. Once when I looked at her, she was leaning back against the tree, her head back, and she was looking up at the moss that hung like coarse spiderweb from the oak's sagging branches. Her eyes were wide and staring, and she looked almost afraid. Then I realized she had lowered her eyes and had caught me watching her. I turned away, looked at the pond, and wished she would go away.

She began to speak in a strangely excited way. "Why aren't there any birds out here? You'd think there'd be a lot of birds in woods like this by a pond. It's so quiet. How do you stand it if you come here every day like you say you do? It's so queer and quiet. It gives me the shivers! It's almost like there was something real bad here, like the evil the priests are always talking about."

I jammed my crude stylus at the ground, and it broke. She laughed—a cruel, hard, hysterical laughter that seemed to echo back from the top of the oak and hover over the pond. I looked at the broken stick and listened to her laughing. I became frightened and ashamed. I jumped up and ran away into the woods. As I ran, it seemed the trees were laughing. For as long as I could hear the laughter, I ran. I followed the edge of the pond, yet I stayed far enough away from it and into the woods that I couldn't see the water. I realized suddenly she was still, and I stopped running. In the quiet, the wood was different. The trees were like animals frozen in their places, threatening to come to life, their limbs trying to catch and strangle me. A small brown rabbit rushed past me, running as if it thought a rabbit-devil were loose in the wood. The sun was well over the tops of the trees, and the heat was more intense, unmitigated by the distant pond or the shade, which, together, had always before placated the sun. I stood a long time, half-frightened and half-curious, wondering what she was doing.

After what seemed a very long time, I was surprised to hear a splash in the pond. I went through the wood as quietly and as quickly as I could. I soon realized I had walked and run nearly all the way around the pond. I went the rest of the way and came into the back of the clearing beneath the oak. She was standing at the edge and throwing dead branches and twigs into the water. A pile of small branches she had collected lay on the bank at her feet. She picked up two at a time and threw first one and then the other into the pond before she stopped to pick up two more. She threw them hard as though she was trying to beat something that wasn't there; and all the time, she made a funny sound. Her shoulders shook when she stopped to watch a stick hit the water, and she breathed in hard and loud, sounding as if she were choking. When the pile of sticks was gone, she turned to look for something else to throw. The sticks floated, black in the water, bobbing without pattern or direction, dead on the surface of the pond. Then she saw me and started shouting at me, crying all the time.

"Why don't they sink? Why? Why don't they? I threw them in because I wanted them to sink! Old pieces of wood! Rotten! Rotten! No-good sticks. Why why why don't they sink?"

She looked so terrible standing there. Her face was wet and dirt-streaked from crying. She looked so terrible and, I thought, so stupid. Mud and bark from the sticks had fallen on the front of her white blouse, leaving it splotched with black and gray. She looked dirty, as if she had crawled on the ground searching for her sticks.

I shouted back at her, "Why are you throwing all those sticks in there? Why are you so stupid? Stupid girl. You're making the pond all dirty. Don't do that, you dirty, stupid girl!"

"Don't call me that! Don't don't don't! I'm not not not dirty! Don't call me dirty! Don't!"

She saw a small stick, jumped for it, and picked it up. She threw it at me, but I ducked. She turned and ran from the clearing and out of sight into the woods. I listened to her crying and running through the brush. I'm sure she fell once. Her crying made it seem almost as though I could hear her running, stumbling, falling, getting up, and running some more. Her crying was like her laugh had been earlier. The trees seemed to hold it down, to shelter it, to magnify it, to distort it until it became hard to tell that it wasn't the wood itself crying. Suddenly, she appeared again by the pond.

She stopped at the end of the fallen pecan tree and looked out toward the blackened stump in the water. Her body still shook hard, but she was quiet. She looked spent, as though she had cried herself dry, and her body shook as a reflex run away from the stimulus. Then she startled me by climbing out on the old tree, moving carefully on her hands and knees toward the stump. Several times, I thought she would fall into the water. She crawled and then started crying so hard she had to stop; and when she could, she crawled again until she started crying again. I knew there were hidden stumps under the fallen-tree bridge that could hurt her if she fell. A couple of times, I started to shout at her and tell her to go back. But I couldn't. I was afraid that if I yelled, I would make her fall. I couldn't do anything but watch her. She finally made it to the stump and stood up as much as she dared. She looked at the water and then at me, and then she started shouting at me again. I hated her when she shouted at me.

"You'll be sorry! Do you hear? Listen! You'll be sorry! They'll all be sorry they called me dirty! I'm not not not. I'm not!"

Before I could shout anything back, she jumped into the pond and disappeared. Then her head came up above the water, away from the stump and out in the clear and deepest area of the pond. She disappeared again and almost as quickly reappeared, this time rising far out of the water as though she were climbing out on the spray she was making before she fell back again to where only her head showed above the pond. Her hair was darkened and strung down in her face. She splashed wildly and shouted for me to help her, but I couldn't. I couldn't move. I could only stand there and watch her disappear and reappear again. This time, she came up, and her eyes looked as I thought a crazy person's should—only scared, crazy wild, and scared. She screamed, and then she went under again. I waited for her to come back. I waited and waited, but she didn't return. She stayed away, somewhere under the pond, and the woods grew stiller than it had ever been. I waited and watched the water where she had last appeared, expecting her to break through the calm surface again. I waited, and I wished I could hear her strange, cruel laugh again.

I can't remember where I spent the rest of the day. When I realized she was never to appear again, I left the pond and the woods. I must have walked all afternoon. When I came into the backyard, the sun had gone behind the trees that lined the highway west of town. There was a light in the kitchen. My mother and sister moved around, setting supper on the table. My father's back was visible as he sat in his usual place, waiting for the food to be served. I knew he would be angry with me for staying away all day, but I thought maybe—if he were tired and hungry enough—he wouldn't hit me. As I went close to the house, I heard him talking to my mother.

"Where is he?" my father asked.

"How should I know? He stays gone all day, doesn't tell me where he's going, and you come in and ask me where he is. How should I know? Tell me! How can I know where that boy goes and what he does?"

"All right, stop your shouting. You can't shout and serve supper at the same time. Stop shouting! I'll ask him where he's been when he gets here."

I waited a moment in the dark under the window, trying to think of a way out, but it was no use. I had to go in. When I opened the door, they all turned to look at me. Mother started to say something but changed her mind. No one spoke as I went to the sink, washed my hands, and then sat in my place at the table. Mother finished placing the food on the table and sat down opposite me. I kept my eyes down, fixed on the chipped edge of my plate. My father, not shouting but speaking loudly, said, "Now that you're here, you going to say grace so we can eat or not?"

"In the name of the Father and of the Son and . . ." I said the grace quickly and inattentively, and I then took the bowls that were passed to me and dished the food onto my plate without speaking again. I felt my father watching me, and I wished he would start and get it over with. But he remained silent until he finished eating. Then he leaned forward and tapped me on the arm with his fork. When I looked up, he was waving the fork in my face.

"Where you been?"

"Nowhere," I whispered.

"Where you been?"

"Nowhere." It was all I could do to force the word out.

He dropped the fork on the table, and he hit me on the shoulder with his open hand. I looked down at my plate. I knew my sister was smiling, and my mother was trying to decide whether she was more angry with me for staying away or with him for hitting me.

My father commanded, "Dammit, boy, tell me where you've been!"

"I've been walking—just fooling around and walking."

"Where? Where've you been walking all day?"

"Nowhere. Nowhere special. I just went walking."

"Get up! Get up!"

"Don't hit him again." My mother decided to plead for me.

"I'm not going to hit him. Now go on upstairs and stay there. You can plan on staying home tomorrow."

I went out of the kitchen and started upstairs when he yelled at me again.

"I expect to see you at breakfast. Do you hear?"

He didn't expect an answer, and I went on upstairs. In my room, I undressed in the dark and stretched out across the bed. When I closed my eyes, I saw the quiet, smooth water where the girl had disappeared, and I heard her laughing under the pond. I opened my eyes, and even the old shadows of my darkened room seemed unfamiliar. The night sounds came in the window, and I listened to the crickets. Their singing had always seemed pleasant, but that night, their sound was harsh and defensive, as though they too were afraid and trying to ward off the night and its dreams. I thought, *I cannot tell them. I cannot tell anyone what happened.* I wasn't every minute certain it had happened until I closed my eyes again and I saw the water—the cooling, quiet water. And I heard her laughter, muffled by the water but hard, cruel, hysterical.

The telephone rang downstairs, and I heard my mother come into the living room to answer it. She talked excitedly, and after she hung up and started back into the kitchen, I heard her say something about Mr. Chauvin's niece. I wanted to open my door and try to hear what was being said, but I was unable to get up. After a time, I began not to notice the crickets, and I fell asleep and began to dream. The girl had hold of me and was trying to pull me into the pond, laughing all the time—laughing, crying, shouting, pulling, and grabbing. I fought back, but she kept dragging me closer to the pond. When I was standing on the edge, about to fall and screaming for help, I awoke.

That next day was terrible. At breakfast, I learned that a neighbor, Mrs. Gaudet, had called my mother and told her Mr. Chauvin's niece was missing. My mother talked about nothing else, and my father didn't understand why she was so upset. I excused myself from the breakfast table as quickly as I could and went outside. I spent the morning in the garage, working on the boat I had started to build in the spring. At lunch, I learned they were dragging the pond in search of the girl, and my father said he was going to help. For a moment, it was all I could do to keep from shouting what had happened. But the moment passed, and I ate my lunch as quickly as I could and went out to the shed again. My father came out a little later and asked if I wanted to go with him to the dragging. I said no. He left and I tried to work on the boat, but I could think only of her laughing and jumping and disappearing and coming to the surface and disappearing and laughing.

My father came in late. Supper was already on the table, and when he sat down, I knew they had found her. The meal was silent. My father looked puzzled, like he was working on something he was afraid he might never figure out. He finally spoke to my mother, but more as though he were talking to himself.

"They found her."

"Poor thing," my mother said.

"Yeah. Doc Bodin says she was there since yesterday morning probably. It doesn't make sense."

My mother waited for him to continue. I took the chance of a glance at each of them, but they were not watching me. My father was visibly upset, in a way I had never seen him before. My mother realized he was waiting for her to say something. She spoke softly, "What? What doesn't make sense?"

"How she could've gotten there. All her clothes on and in the middle of the pond. Old Chauvin said she couldn't swim. Only way to get there was for her to climb out on a fallen tree to a stump. But it doesn't make sense."

"If that's the only way, why doesn't it make sense? Poor thing."

My mother stopped and waited. I watched her trying to decide whether or not she should say something more. She obviously decided to say something, but before she could, my father started again.

"What the hell's she doing crawling out to that stump? A young girl. Wearing a dress. Chauvin said she couldn't swim. She had all her clothes on. It doesn't make sense."

My mother interjected, "Poor thing. Maybe it's better."

My father was startled.

"Better! How better? You call being dead better? Than what?"

"Well, this afternoon, I heard she was here because not many people knew her and she was in trouble. I heard—"

"You heard crap. Even if it's true, and I doubt it, that still don't make being dead better. Eat your supper."

The last was aimed at me. I had been listening, unable to eat, barely able to keep myself from jumping up and running out. But the sight of my father's face and the tone of his voice kept me at the table. I forced some of the food down.

My mother asked, "How's Mr. Chauvin?"

"Pretty bad. He's taking it hard. He said he's going to have the pond filled in. Blames himself, saying he should've done it before."

I stopped trying to eat. I felt warm, and the faces around the table became blurred. The voices, asking and answering, seemed muffled suddenly, distorted as though they were far away. I saw the girl jumping, laughing, crawling out on the tree—jumping, laughing, and crying. Why did she do it? Why? I excused myself from the table, saying I didn't feel well and wanted to go to my room. I was surprised there were no protests.

Later, as I lay on the bed in the dark, I heard their voices like echoes coming up from the living room. It was Saturday night, and the music from Gary's Bar was loudly raucous. I turned, and through the window, I watched the moon hide between little patches of cloud only to reappear, hearing her, seeing her, trying to reach her. Why didn't she come back?

I heard my parents come up the stairs and go to bed. They were still talking about her. I listened to the music from Gary's, and then the crickets began to sing again. A dog barked, and from the street, I heard a girl laugh—a new laugh, not like hers, but high, and clear and happy in the night and the moon reminded me of her, hiding, reappearing, sinking, rising, and disappearing. Why did she do it? Why did she stay gone? I lay in the dark, afraid to close my eyes. A soft summer rain fell, but I didn't get up to pull down the window.

I closed my eyes to sleep. The night sounds slowly went away, and then I saw her. I was reaching for her, trying to pull her out, and she was screaming, laughing, and trying to pull me in. There was an enormous pile of dirt and a bulldozer pushing the dirt into the pond, and a lot of people stood around. All of them were laughing. I was crying and trying to tell them not to push the dirt into the pond because she was still there, but no one understood. They all laughed at me. I heard her laughing and screaming. Her eyes were crazy, wild, and afraid; and then there was only the pile of dirt.

All the people had gone away. I didn't hear her laughing for a long time. Then she started again for a moment, and she stopped laughing and started crying a soft and sad cry. I was on top of the pile of dirt. I tried to run away, but I ran and ran. I couldn't get off the pile of dirt, and she was underneath and kept crying. No matter how hard I ran, I heard her soft little-girl cry from underneath the pond and from underneath the dirt. I wanted her to stop, but she wouldn't. I heard her crying every way I turned.

HARMONY'S SONG

HARMONY ROMERO FELT the stares even before she walked through the door of the Fashion Spot. Four men at the bar all turned to watch her as she came in, and her skin tingled as though something was crawling on it. She really did not want to be there, but Eric had insisted. "I need you," he had said.

"You always need me."

"And you're always there. That's what's so great about you."

She thought it was true. It had been true for nearly a year. He said he needed her, and she was always there. She often said she needed him, and he was hard to find. More often than not, he was a recorded voice on an answering machine with a message that made clear he thought of himself as the world's greatest gift to women.

And it usually was at least a whole day or two before he called back.

The latest time he called he said he needed to see her because he had to leave town for a few days—maybe for a week—on business. The rush of sensations brought on by the thought of him being away for a week made her not register that he was telling her to meet him at the Fashion Spot until it was too late. She tried to think of someplace else to meet, but he was already saying "See you at six, Harmony. Ta-ta!" He sang the last two syllables.

She held the phone for a moment and wondered why Eric had chosen the Fashion Spot as a place to meet. Weekend tourists looking for a singles scene in New Orleans thought it was a place to go to, partly because it was in the area known as Fat City. Harmony knew it was really a meat locker, a bar filled with chic plastic décor and a crowd of women in their midtwenties who knew they were on display. Harmony thought some of them should have simply hung a sign around their necks that said "For Rent," to avoid confusion.

She looked along the bar and the row of tables against the wall. Four men sat on stools at the bar. Couples sat at most of the tables. Five women sat around one table, looking, Harmony thought, as if they were trying to figure out how to divide the four men at the bar among themselves. Two of the women glared at her. She was bewildered by the hostility in their faces. She felt an impulse to tell them they need not worry about her. She was meeting someone. He would be here any minute.

At the bar, one of the men stood and made a gesture as though to offer her a stool. He was nice-looking, taller than Eric, and maybe looked younger, but it was hard to be sure in the dim light. He smiled at her. She looked at him and felt the others watching her, then she walked past him to a table in a rear corner and sat facing the door. The man who had offered the stool and the others at the bar were laughing. The five women at the round table looked at her then turned away. One of them muttered something that started them all giggling. Harmony tried to ignore them, but the high tilted mirror that ran the length of the wall behind the bar reflected everything in the room.

Her own image in the mirror startled her, with her hair down, falling almost to her shoulder blades, and her face with the dark glasses still on. She took off the glasses and put them in her purse. A waitress appeared at the table, and Harmony told her she was waiting for someone. She would order when he arrived.

The men at the bar laughed again. One of them slapped the bar several times with his open hand, and even the bartender moved closer to try to get in on the fun. Harmony heard one of the men ask, "Is she a new one?"

The bartender shook his head and squinted through the dim light toward her. Harmony had been there only a few times with Eric. She did not remember the bartender. She couldn't tell how well he was able to see her. He shook his head side to side again and leaned forward to whisper something to the other men.

They laughed, and the one who had stood earlier to offer her a stool turned and looked at her. Where was Eric? The man was definitely younger and taller than Eric. He walked toward her in a way that made her think he was easily impressed with himself. She stood and looked around. She then followed the sign to the ladies' room, hearing the word *fox* and louder laughter at the bar as she pushed through the restroom door.

She touched up her lipstick, recombed her hair, and made sure her blouse was straight. When he had called, Eric's voice had had a special pleading in it that she had learned to recognize, and she had dressed for him. She was feeling like an idiot for letting him put her in a situation that made her run to the ladies' room to hide. She studied herself in the mirror and thought about the last time they had met, when she told Eric she didn't want to see him again.

He had called the next night with a pleading tone in his voice and asked her to meet him at the Café du Monde at ten. She waited at one of the small, round, marble-top tables until almost eleven, until she had been asked to order something or leave. She remembered the embarrassment that had flooded through her and how she had sworn she would never wait for him again. He arrived as she was getting up to leave. She remembered how remorseful he had been and how especially tender he had been later that night at his apartment.

Of course, she thought, he was late again, and she fully expected him to be there when she came back to her table. She stood holding on to a chair and looked around the room. Harmony felt helpless and paralyzed when she looked around the room and saw that Eric still wasn't there.

The waitress approached Harmony and asked, "Are you all right?"

"I'm fine. Is there another way out of here?"

"This way," the waitress said and pointed down the narrow hall that led to the restrooms. "Take a right at the end and you'll see the exit sign. It leads out to the parking lot in back."

Harmony hesitated and looked back to the bar. Two different men had replaced the three who had been there when she arrived. The change made her feel confused.

The waitress said, "Maybe he'll come in a minute."

"What?"

"The one you're waiting for. Maybe he'll show up in a minute."

Harmony said, "He's not coming." Then she asked, "Is there a pay phone?"

The waitress pointed again down the hall toward the back.

Harmony followed the hall and found the phone on the wall next to the rear exit. She rummaged in her purse to find a coin, dialed Eric's number, and waited. It rang three times, then there was a click and a whirring sound followed by the answering machine playing Eric's greeting.

"This is Eric Andrepont. I can't come to the phone now, but at the tone, leave your name, age, measurements, and phone number, and I'll call you as soon as I have a clear spot on my calendar. Ta-ta."

Harmony had once told Eric that the message offended her. He had laughed and had said it was only a joke.

She said, "Eric, I'm at the Fashion Spot. I can't wait in this place. If you really want to see me, I'll be at home."

She hung up and went out the rear door to the parking lot. The air had turned gray and was full of a fine mist. She didn't have an umbrella and had to walk through an alley to get to the street. By the time she got to her car, she was wet, cold, and mad.

When she drove into the lot of her apartment complex, she looked around to see if his car was parked in the visitors' parking area. It wasn't. In her apartment, she immediately felt its emptiness. He was not there. She hadn't consciously expected him to be, but the sense of aloneness still caught her by surprise. She had to stop for a moment and take several deep breaths to smooth out the ragged edges of her nerves.

Harmony took off her wet clothes and put on the jogging suit she usually wore when she expected to stay around the apartment. She fixed a light supper and watched television. She tried to read three or four of the magazines on the coffee table, but she gave that up when she realized she was looking at the pictures without registering anything about them. She called Eric's number three times, but all she heard was the beginning of the same recorded message. She hung up each time as soon as the tape began to play.

She remembered the less-than-half-full bottle of wine left in the refrigerator from a week before, when Eric had come for dinner. She poured herself a glass and took it with her into the bathroom, where she undressed. She was twenty-seven years old and, she knew, not strikingly beautiful—but she kept herself in shape with aerobics and a reasonable diet. And she knew men were attracted by her dark hair and by a certain breathy quality in her voice.

Several times in recent weeks, Eric had seemed on the verge of telling her something. The morning three days ago especially, after he'd come to dinner and stayed the night, she thought he was about to say something; then he realized he had to hurry and leave or be late for work. Harmony finished drinking the glass of wine before getting into the shower. She hadn't finished drying herself when the phone rang.

In the middle of Harmony's hello, Eric said, "Sorry about this afternoon. I got tied up."

Harmony said, "You do that a lot."

"Don't get huffed about it."

"You know I hate that place."

"I said I'm sorry. Can I come over?"

"No."

"Why not?"

She looked at the digital clock on her dresser and saw it was nearly ten. "It's too late. I'm tired and I have to get up early tomorrow."

"Tomorrow's Sunday. You never get up early on Sunday."

Harmony took a deep breath. He was right. She felt a little chill that told her she was weakening. Then she thought of the one thing that was sure to work.

"I'm going to see my mother."

Her mother lived in Lafayette, almost a three-hour drive from New Orleans. Eric had already dodged making the trip to see her mother several times. Harmony made the trip every six or seven weeks. She had not planned on going to her mother's this weekend. "Besides," she said, "I thought you were going out of town."

Eric said, "Change in plans. I'm going next weekend. So if you want to see me, I better come over tonight."

"No, Eric. I'll come back early tomorrow. I'll call you then."

Eric hung up with his usual "ta-ta."

Harmony finished dressing for bed, turned off the lights, opened the draperies, and raised a window. It was April, but the evenings were still cool. A television weatherman had said it was the coolest spring in decades for southern Louisiana. She got into bed and looked out the window. The sky was clear and full of stars.

Eric knew all about the stars. He had tried to help her find the Big and Little Dippers, Orion, and other constellations; but when she looked at the sky, all she saw was a dark sky full of stars. Eric had become impatient and told her he wouldn't try to teach her anything else.

A mockingbird in the trees behind the apartment sang. Harmony knew that sound because when she was a young girl, a mockingbird had made a nest in the oak tree in her backyard. Her mother had told her that the night song was the male singing out of his need for the female. She thought of Eric trying to tell her something that he couldn't get out.

She turned on the lamp beside her bed and dialed his number. She heard the phone ring three times before Eric's message voice said, "Hi, this is Eric. I just stepped out for a minute. I'll be back soon, so just leave a number. Ta-ta."

Harmony rushed her words out. "Eric, I'm sorry I was so cold. When you come back, don't go away again. I'm on my way over, as soon as I get dressed. Ta-ta!"

She sang the sign-off.

She acted quickly. She didn't need makeup; an old dress would be all right. Her hair needed combing, but Eric wouldn't mind. He'd be happy just to see her. And if Eric hadn't returned yet, she had her own key.

During the day, the trip from Harmony's apartment to Eric's could take thirty-five or forty minutes. At this time of night—without traffic and with a little luck with green lights—she made it in just over twenty.

Eric's car was in its usual parking space, and she parked her car next to his. His apartment was dark. She rang his doorbell several times, but he didn't answer. Sounds of loud music and laughter and voices came from an apartment on the other side of the small courtyard that served as a common patio for the dozen apartments that surrounded it. Harmony found her key in her purse and was opening Eric's door when the music and voices got louder and light splashed onto the courtyard from the opened door of the noisy apartment. A woman laughed, and a man answered with laughter that Harmony recognized.

Eric said, "Let's try my place."

The woman said, "We shouldn't."

"Of course we should. You liked it there last time. Not to mention the time before and the time—"

"Hush. Aren't you the one who's always talking about being discreet?"

Their laughter came closer, and Harmony looked for some place to hide. Eric and the woman—a blonde—stepped from the shadows in a splash of light in the courtyard. There was no place for Harmony to escape except into Eric's apartment. She jumped inside and shut and relocked the door behind her. She hurried through the living room into the second bedroom, which Eric used as an office. She left a small crack in the door, just enough to hear through, and knelt on the floor behind Eric's desk. The front door opened and closed. A soft light came through the small opening at the door.

Eric said, "Wine?"

The woman must have nodded yes. There was the sound of the wine being poured and of glasses being clinked together.

Harmony felt a mixture of anger and humiliation rising up in her so strongly it seemed to her that Eric and the woman should have been able to sense it. He had told Harmony he needed her. He had never said he loved her, but at those times recently when he seemed near to saying something, she believed he had come close. He had acted like he might love her. He really had.

The woman said, "I want another glass."

Eric said, "Don't get sloshed on me. It's a lot more fun when you know what you're doing."

"One more."

Again Harmony heard someone moving around.

Eric said, "My message light is on."

"Let it go."

"I don't like to ignore messages. You never know when it might be important."

Harmony heard her own voice. Although most of the words weren't distinct, she heard herself singing "ta-ta."

Eric said, "Damn!"

"What's the matter?"

"You have to go, my love."

"What do you mean?"

"What I said, love. Harmony's on her way over here. The girl I told you has been pestering me. You've got to be a good girl and disappear. Go back to the party, or go upstairs to your place. I'll get rid of her and come for you. It won't take long, but she's going to be here any minute—you've got to go."

The woman said, "I thought you were going to tell her to get out of your life."

"I am, love. I am. I'm looking for the right moment. She's a sweet kid, and I don't want to hurt her any more than I have to."

"If you can't tell her, I can."

"I'll do it. Come on, you've got to go. I'll come for you after I've gotten rid of Harmony."

Harmony bit her lip and tasted blood. Her eyes filled, and the very air in the room seemed to attack her flesh. She thought of how she had deluded herself about what he had been trying to say. She clenched her fists and leaned her forehead on the desk. She fought down the scream swelling up inside her.

From the other room came the sound of a slap. The woman said, "Don't pat me there and tell me you're waiting for another woman."

"Don't be difficult, love."

"If I'm your love, meet her at the door and tell her you're with someone else."

"I can't do it that way. Harmony's too sweet."

"Don't push me," the woman said.

"You've got to go."

"No, I don't."

There was the sound of another slap, only this time it was a sharper sound of flesh against flesh, hard. Someone—or something—fell.

"You bastard."

"Don't call me names, love. Just get the hell out of here."

"You're going to have to throw me out."

"Suit yourself."

Harmony listened to Eric and the woman fighting. The sounds got louder then diminished, as though they had moved from the living room to the kitchen. Both were yelling. Objects fell, maybe a lamp or a couple of lamps, with the sound of glass breaking. Harmony stood and moved to the door, trying to see through the crack.

"You bastard," the woman said again.

"Put that down."

Sounds of movement, maybe scuffling, then the sound of someone sucking in air and pushing it out again. Something heavy fell. The woman shouted, "Oh my god."

Eric said, "Get help. Quick." There was something wrong with his voice. He made gurgling noises.

Harmony opened the door and moved cautiously into the living room. Beyond, in the kitchen, the blond woman, who was very pretty, stood over Eric, who lay on the floor with a large kitchen knife stuck in his abdomen. The woman was wiping blood from her hands onto her blouse. All the buttons on her blouse were undone.

"Help me!" Eric said. His voice was weaker.

The blonde turned and ran from the apartment. Harmony watched her go, leaving the front door open. The woman's high heels rapped sharply on the paved walk, then on the stairs and along the balcony that allowed entrance to the second-floor apartments. A door slammed. All got quiet. Harmony thought the whole world was the quietest it had ever been. Harmony went to the kitchen and leaned over Eric.

"Harmony," he said, seeing her. "Thank God you're here. Call an ambulance, please."

Harmony bent over him, but not within reach, and she was careful to avoid stepping in the growing puddle of blood. Eric's shirt and the top of his pants were soaked with it. It covered his hands and ran onto the floor. The look in his eyes was changing from intense pain and fear to a slowly growing cloudiness. As she watched his face turn gray, she thought of herself hiding in the study, listening to the laughter and the wineglasses clinking together. "Harmony," she heard him saying. "I'll get rid of her. I'll come for you." The woman's blouse had been unbuttoned. Had it gotten that way in their scuffle? Or had Eric unbuttoned the woman's blouse on the sofa before he went to get the second glass of wine?

"Harmony," he whispered.

"I'm here, Eric." She said it softly, almost tenderly, but she didn't touch him.

She watched him until he closed his eyes. His breathing came hard, with long spaces between breaths. Then she got to her feet. Stepping carefully around the blood, she found the answering machine and ran it back to where her message to him began. She erased it, looked back once at Eric, and left, closing the door behind her. She did not lock it.

In the parking lot, she looked up at the apartments on the second floor. Lights were on in most of them, and she had no idea which one the blonde had run to. Was the woman trying to wash Eric's blood off her hands and out of her blouse? The party across the courtyard was still going on.

*   *   *

The clock on her dresser read 1:46. She was surprised she had been gone so long. She changed again for bed, turned out the light, and looked out at the clear, dark sky full of stars. Harmony leaned over and dialed Eric's number. She listened to his recorded message then said, "This is Harmony. I wanted to tell you good night, Eric, and to say I'm sorry I missed you tonight. Call me again, anytime." And softly and tenderly, she said, "Ta-ta, Eric. Ta-ta."

ACKNOWLEDGMENTS

The following stories have been previously published:

"A Wide Day." *Blue Lake Review* (January 2013). Bluelakereview.weebly.com.

"All in a Day's Work." *Hudson Review*, 42 (Winter 1990): 549–564.

"Harmony's Song." *Ellery Queen's Mystery Magazine*, 92.3 (1988): 128–37.

"Ramblers and Spinners." *Hudson Review*, 40 (1988): 561–83.

"Picking Up the Pieces" ("The Auctioneer" original title). *Sun Dog*, 5 (1984): 58–66. Republished in *Something in Common: An Anthology of Louisiana Writers*, edited by Ann Brewster Dobie. Louisiana State University Press (1991), 241–252.

"The Tick Is Full." *Hudson Review*, 37 (1984): 399–420.

"The Chill." *Cuyahoga Review*, 1 (1983): 155–65.

""Final Arrangements." *Ball State University Forum*, 8 (1967): 17–22.

"That Summer Day" Literary Review, 9 (1965): 65-76.

"A Boy in the Woods," Take a Mind Walk (Scribes Valley Press) 2018.

CPSIA information can be obtained
at www.ICGtesting.com
Printed in the USA
FSHW012216160219
55721FS